Readers love ANDREW GREY

The Viscount's Rancher

"Andrew Grey fans will be very happy how it turns out, and romance fans in general will be as well."

—Love Bytes

The Northern Lights in His Eyes

"If you love second chances, friends to lovers, hurt/comfort, beautiful settings, close friends, small towns, slow burn, cute dogs, suspense and a HEA... go get this book!"

—TTC Books and More

"This book was sweet, steamy and well written and just the right length to give us a well rounded story"

—MM Romance Reviewed

"The pull between the two men is well-done and their issues give them conflict. And the HEA ending satisfied."

—Sparkling Book Reviews

Love at First Swipe

"Darby and Reynaldo were wonderful, caring and loving characters who deserve a HEA, but I won't reveal if they get it or not. Of course, if you are a fan of Mr. Grey you already know."

—Paranormal Romance Guild

"This was a really sweet love story a bit like a warm hug, and the best thing is there is an app like this that really exists!!"

—Love Bytes

By Andrew Grey (cont.)

CARLISLE DEPUTIES
Fire and Flint • Fire and Granite
Fire and Agate • Fire and Obsidian
Fire and Onyx • Fire and Diamond

CARLISLE FIRE
Through the Flames

CARLISLE TROOPERS
Fire and Sand • Fire and Glass
Fire and Ermine

CHEMISTRY
Organic Chemistry • Biochemistry
Electrochemistry • Chemistry
Anthology

COWBOY NOBILITY
The Duke's Cowboy
The Viscount's Rancher

DREAMSPUN DESIRES
The Lone Rancher
Poppy's Secret
The Best Worst Honeymoon Ever

EYES OF LOVE
Eyes Only for Me • Eyes Only for You

FOREVER YOURS
Can't Live Without You
Never Let You Go

GOOD FIGHT
The Good Fight • The Fight Within
The Fight for Identity
Takoda and Horse

HEARTS ENTWINED
Heart Unseen • Heart Unheard
Heart Untouched • Heart Unbroken

HOLIDAY STORIES
Copping a Sweetest Day Feel
Cruise for Christmas
Frosty the Schnauzer
A Lion in Tails • Mariah the
Christmas Moose
A Present in Swaddling Clothes
Rudolph the Rescue Jack Russell
Secret Guncle • Simple Gifts
Snowbound in Nowhere
Stardust • Sweet Anticipation
With Amy Lane: Holiday Cheer Anthology

LAS VEGAS ESCORTS
The Price • The Gift

LOVE MEANS…
Love Means… No Shame
Love Means… Courage
Love Means… No Boundaries
Love Means… Freedom
Love Means … No Fear
Love Means… Healing
Love Means… Family
Love Means… Renewal
Love Means… No Limits
Love Means… Patience
Love Means… Endurance

LOVE'S CHARTER
Setting the Hook • Ebb and Flow

Published by Dreamspinner Press
www.dreamspinnerpress.com

By ANDREW GREY (CONT.)

MUST LOVE DOGS
Frosty the Schnauzer
Rescue Me • Rescue Us
Rudolph the Rescue Jack Russell
Secret Guncle

NEW LEAF ROMANCES
New Leaf • In the Weeds

PAINT BY NUMBER
Paint By Number • The Northern
Lights in His Eyes

PLANTING DREAMS
Planting His Dream • Growing His
Dream

REKINDLED FLAME
Rekindled Flame • Cleansing Flame
Smoldering Flame

SENSES
Love Comes Silently
Love Comes in Darkness
Love Comes Home
Love Comes Around
Love Comes Unheard
Love Comes to Light

SEVEN DAYS
Seven Days • Unconditional Love

STORIES FROM THE RANGE
A Shared Range • A Troubled Range
An Unsettled Range • A Foreign Range
An Isolated Range • A Volatile Range
A Chaotic Range

STRANDED
Stranded • Taken

TALES FROM KANSAS
Dumped in Oz • Stuck in Oz
Trapped in Oz

TALES FROM ST. GILES
Taming the Beast
Redeeming the Stepbrother

TASTE OF LOVE
A Taste of Love • A Serving of Love
A Helping of Love • A Slice of Love

WITHOUT BORDERS
A Heart Without Borders
A Spirit Without Borders

WORK OUT
Spot Me • Pump Me Up • Core Training
Crunch Time • Positive Resistance
Personal Training • Cardio Conditioning
Work Me Out Anthology

Published by DREAMSPINNER PRESS
www.dreamspinnerpress.com

STEAL MY *Heart*

ANDREW GREY

Published by
DREAMSPINNER PRESS

8219 Woodville Hwy #1245
Woodville, FL 32362 USA
www.dreamspinnerpress.com

This is a work of fiction. Names, characters, places, and incidents either are the product of author imagination or are used fictitiously, and any resemblance to actual persons, living or dead, business establishments, events, or locales is entirely coincidental.

Steal My Heart
© 2024 Andrew Grey

Cover Art
© 2024 L.C. Chase
http://www.lcchase.com
Cover content is for illustrative purposes only and any person depicted on the cover is a model.

Trade Paperback ISBN: 978-1-64108-711-7
Digital ISBN: 978-1-64108-710-0
Trade Paperback published November 2024
v. 1.0

To Karen for the setting and help with the research, and to Dominic for all his support. And to Christine—you're in my thoughts.

Chapter 1

"WHAT THE hell?" Hilliard almost dropped the box he was carrying up to what he hoped would be his office. Out in front of his house, two small dogs were barking like their lives were in danger. He set down the box and nearly fell down the stairs as he hurried to the front door, the barking getting louder with every step. "What's going on?" The door nearly fell off its hinges as he burst out into the tiny yard, where a man lay tangled in leashes at the edge of the road just outside the picket fence. His two yippy terriers nearly came unglued at Hilliard's appearance.

"Gigi, Poppy, stop," the man said as he sat up and tried to get his legs out of the leashes. The two dogs bounded to him as soon as he was free, running in happy circles that threatened to tangle him up all over again.

"Are you all right?" Hilliard asked. The dogs ran over to him and jumped against his legs as though he might have treats for them.

"I'm fine, but these two hellions are going to kill me, I swear." The man managed to get the leashes untwisted and one in each hand as he tried to keep the two manic dogs apart.

"Are you sure?" A trail of blood ran down the man's leg below his shorts. "I think you need to clean that up."

The man looked down and went pale.

Hilliard hurried inside and returned with a wet cloth, which he handed to the man, who used it to wipe up the blood. He still seemed unsteady.

"It's just a small cut, nothing to be too worried about. Make sure you wash it well when you get home."

"Thanks. I'll be okay. It's not that far," he said and continued slowly down the road. Hilliard watched him go, because at the moment, other than marshaling the few boxes he'd brought with him, he had nothing else to do.

Well, that wasn't exactly true. The tiny yard needed attention, and the house needed repairs and painting. He needed to get up on a ladder to see if he had to have the roof replaced, and Hilliard was pretty sure the hot water heater was on its last legs. So technically, he had a ton of things he needed to get his butt doing.

He closed the gate, and chips of paint fell off the fence to the sidewalk. Great—another thing to add to the list. That is if he decided to stay. God, right now he needed a glass of wine, some soft jazz, and maybe a damned good fuck. But he was out of wine and there was no place to buy it in town at this time of the night short of going to Fort Bragg, he hadn't unpacked his collection of vinyl, and his boyfriend of eight years was back in fucking Cleveland, probably fucking the goddamned fucking guy who had cut their lawn for the past three years. So in short, he was shit out of luck.

Hilliard finished lugging in the last of the boxes and got them in their rooms. Then he sat in the living room in the old-lady chair with the doily over the back. That lasted about three minutes before he got up again and started pulling doilies off everything. He unpacked the living room boxes and repacked them with things he would never use, including dozens of lace table covers, knickknacks of every possible description, and enough throw blankets to cover half the small town. He wasn't sure what to do with those boxes. Maybe one of the local churches would have a tag sale he could donate them to.

By the time it was dark, Hilliard had the windows open, and the sound of the ocean drifted in on the night fog. He still had the bedroom to set up, so he headed upstairs to the front room and got to work.

BARKING WOKE him the following morning. Hilliard cracked his eyes open, got up, and pushed the curtains aside, peering down to the front of the house, where the same man tried not to get tangled in the leashes… again. Gigi and Poppy were in fine form, bounding everywhere, yapping, tails wagging a mile a minute. It took him about ten seconds standing in the open window before he remembered he was naked and probably flashing half of Mendocino. He jumped back, and the curtains fell into place. He didn't hear any screaming or laughing, so maybe he hadn't been seen.

He checked the time and groaned before pulling on a pair of light black sweatpants and a red Cleveland jersey and heading downstairs. He needed coffee badly, and maybe a chance to wake up. He brewed some and poured himself a cup, then headed out front to his small porch, where a wicker chair sat to one side. He sat down and promptly went through the seat, spilling coffee all over the floorboards.

"And I thought I was graceful," the man said, coming from the opposite direction he had earlier, the dogs a little more sedate.

Hilliard managed to get out of the chair and stacked it with the pile of trash he seemed to be collecting along the side of the house. "I guess we're two of a kind. Though you probably have one over on me. At least the dogs have minds of their own." He smiled and got one in return. "They seem quieter." He approached the fence and pushed open the gate. The dogs came right in, accepting all the attention he was willing to give them.

"And you seem a lot more… dressed." That smile became a grin.

Hilliard colored, his cheeks heating. "Sorry."

Damned if that smile didn't stay in place. "Don't be on my account." Hilliard might have gotten a wink, but he wasn't sure. One of the dogs, probably Gigi, decided to go in for a kiss and nearly knocked him off-balance. She bounded back as though she was checking her handiwork.

"Come on, little miss, we need to leave him alone so he can have some coffee, and I need to get you home so I can get to work." The man flashed another smile and set off down the street. This time Hilliard groaned to himself as he watched him go, a pair of tight shorts hugging a perfect backside. If there were music, he could sing along with him and follow the bouncing buttcheeks. All he could think was he sure as hell was not in Cleveland anymore.

TWO DAYS later, Hilliard was sitting in a new chair he'd gotten at the Fort Bragg Home Depot, waiting for the handyman. He'd gotten the living room set up and even painted his bedroom. Two rooms down, several to go. He had a small dining room, the kitchen, and the second bedroom, as well as his office, to finish working on. Oh, he almost forgot—by the time he went through the bathroom and threw away all the pill bottles, both empty and full, and half-full bottles of toiletries, he'd found a room in good shape in light green. All it needed was a thorough cleaning and he was set to go. But beyond that, he needed help.

He'd called a number of people in the area, but he'd only gotten voicemail and no callbacks. At the end of the list, he called and a lady answered the phone. She took his information and actually made an appointment for someone to come by this morning. Now if the handyperson actually showed up, it would be some kind of miracle. There were many things he could do, but heavy maintenance was not one of them. At least he had managed to get the old lawnmower that had been lodged in the tiny shed out back running, so he'd cut the grass.

At almost exactly eight, as promised, a red van pulled up in front of the house. Hilliard smiled as someone got out and came around to the gate, which promptly fell off its hinges as soon as he opened it. "I'm sorry," Hilliard said as he hurried out. "It's you." The leash-tangled dog man smiled. Damn, he found himself grinning like an idiot. "Where are the dogs?"

"They don't come to work with me. I'd never get anything done." Damn, was it possible to be hotter in coveralls and a T-shirt than in tight shorts? Hilliard thought so. Maybe it was the hints of what was underneath, with the shirt stretched over his chest and the way his waist disappeared into the fitted green overalls. "I'm Brian Mayer." He held out his hand.

"Hilliard Bauman, though my friends call me Hill."

"Not Hilly?" he asked, and Hilliard fake scowled. "Okay, Hill." He kept that smile in place. "What is it you need done?"

"What *doesn't* need fixing? I think the place has had a good ten years of delayed maintenance. I know it needs paint, but I'm afraid to do that until I know that the rest of it isn't falling apart underneath. The front door seems wonky, the water heater is cranky, and God knows what else. I'm a little afraid to turn things on."

Brian nodded. "I get that, but believe me, I've seen worse. Grace was a nice lady, but she was old."

"Did you know my great-aunt?" Hilliard asked as he leaned the gate against the fence.

"I did." Brian looked around. "This is a small town, so just about everyone knows everyone else in one way or another." He lifted his gaze upward. "I always loved this house, with the ornate trim and the widow's walk on the roof. This is one of the older homes in town, and it has plenty of character."

It did have that. "I came here a few times when I was a kid with my grandmother. I have vague but happy memories of Aunt Grace, though I hadn't seen her in quite a while." Honestly, he had thought she'd died years ago. No one in the family talked about her much, at least not after Gran died. He never understood that.

"How about I start inside with the water heater and the furnace? Let me check those out, and then I'll look at the door and gate, as well as the rest of the outside. Do you want me to check the roof?"

"Please. I need to know what's going to require work so I can put together a plan. Some of it I can do myself, but there is some stuff that I can't." And he needed a place where he could have some peace and quiet.

"I see," Brian said.

"Alan, my ex…." Thank God they hadn't gotten married. Hilliard knew he had dodged a bullet there. They had been talking about it and were even looking at rings, but now he knew those plans had been a way for Alan to trap him. "He was handy around the house and could fix anything."

"All right, why don't I get started? It will take me about an hour to look things over, and then we can go from there."

"Great. I have some coffee or water if you'd like some," Hilliard offered. He handed Brian a cold bottle of water, then let him get to work.

Hilliard wasn't going to follow him around, looking over his shoulder, so he went upstairs to work on his office. Fortunately it wasn't wallpapered. Hilliard was dreading the dining room, with that blocky flowered paper that had probably been up fifty years or more. The room upstairs was mostly storage, and he had already hauled everything out. He'd hoped to come across something interesting, but no such luck. There had been no hidden gems in the pile of crap. He did find out that his aunt loved romance novels. He'd even found signed books, which he transferred to the shelves in the living room, removing tons of paperbacks to make space. His plan was to donate them all.

Part of him felt bad that he was removing his aunt from the house. This was all that was left of her, and it felt like he was evicting her one room at a time. Maybe he could think of a way to keep her memory alive in the house, but for now, he needed a functional office space, which meant cleaning and painting.

"Hill?" Brian's warm voice drifted up the stairs. Hill put his cloth aside and went down to meet him. "I have good news and some bad news. The water heater is nearly toast, and I'm surprised it hasn't sprung a leak already. The furnace just needs a good cleaning and it will be ready to go, though. I can handle both of those for you."

"Excellent." Hilliard tried to keep his mind on what Brian was saying, but his attention wandered, along with his gaze.

"The roof is only ten years old, so it's in good shape, no troubles there. I can fix the front door and the gate. The fence needs to be painted. The outside of the house needs to be cleaned and painted, as you expected. The porch in front is good, but the steps are a hazard and need to be rebuilt."

Hilliard nodded. That wasn't as bad as he had feared. "So can you do all that?"

"Of course," Brian said.

"Okay. When can you start?" Hilliard asked, anxious to get started but figuring he would need to wait his turn.

Brian cleared his throat. "Right away." He suddenly seemed nervous.

"Don't you have other clients?" Hilliard asked. "I would suspect that a handyman would be really busy."

"I just finished up a job and have a hole in my calendar, so I can get started." He went to the truck and returned with a clipboard. "These are my rates. I do good work, and I don't waste time. I believe my customers should get a good value. I keep my receipts for supplies and charge you accordingly." Hilliard reviewed the document, which detailed the work Brian was going to do and his hourly rate. Then Hilliard signed the order, and he got right to work, which pleased Hilliard. Brian's plan was to fix what he could today, and then tomorrow he'd get the new water heater and the supplies for the steps and install them.

Hilliard loaded the car with things he planned to donate, then dropped the books at the library for their sale room and drove to the church, where he hauled in four boxes that the church ladies seemed thrilled to get.

"You're Grace's nephew?" one of the ladies asked.

"Her great-nephew, yes." He wasn't sure why he was being so exact.

"I'm Ruth. She and I were friends for many years." Her hands shook, but her eyes were warm and bright. "Good friends, and I remember you." That took Hilliard by surprise. "You were about eight or nine when you visited. We walked you out to the end of the point because I said that sometimes there were seals and you wanted to see them."

"Yes. I remember that. Auntie held my hand because she was afraid I was going to get too close to the edge." He smiled. That had been a long time ago.

"Yes. Grace was always cautious. Are you staying in the house?"

"Yes. I'm working to get it back into shape." He was still trying to decide if he was going to stay here or fix up the house to sell it.

"I know a good handyman if you need some help," one of the other ladies said, verbally muscling in on the conversation.

"I'm sure Hilliard's man is more than capable, Violet," Ruth said in a fake sugary tone that seemed to go right over Violet's head.

"Stevensons are the people I use. They're out of Fort Bragg, but they do good work. I can give you their number if you need it."

Hilliard shook his head. "No, thanks. I already have someone. Brian Mayer is at the house now." He smiled until Violet's expression fell, and then she put her hand over her mouth.

"No," she said, leaning closer. "You left him at the house alone?" She clicked her teeth softly.

"Violet Trainer, that's enough. You know being gossipy is not your best trait." Dang, Ruth had some teeth and was ready to use them. "The boxes Hilliard brought in need to be sorted."

Violet cleared her throat like she was going to persist, but turned and strode away.

"I take it there's a story there," Hilliard said.

Ruth nodded. "But it's not ours to tell," she said more loudly, meeting Violet's gaze until the other lady lowered hers and got busy. "I'm sure everything is going to be fine and you have nothing to worry about." She took his arm and guided him out of the church and away from prying ears. "When you go through things, make sure you look closely before throwing anything out. Grace could be squirrely, especially these last few years."

"She may have hidden things?" Hilliard asked.

Ruth nodded. "Yes. From her son, Timothy." She made that sucking-a-lemon face, and Hilliard couldn't blame her from what he knew of Timothy. "That man was not good to her. The last time I saw him, he and Grace were fighting. Grace and I were going to have lunch, and he was saying hurtful things to her. Anyway, she told me that he had been in the house and that she thought he was looking for things, but that he wasn't going to find anything."

That could mean a lot of things. "I'll be careful and look through everything." Maybe he should have checked through the books, but it was too late now.

Ruth patted his arm and then let go with a smile. Hilliard left the church, stepping out into the misty air, anxious to get home and hating that Violet's comments had gotten to him.

Chapter 2

BRIAN HAD fixed the front door and gate, along with a few of the other small items, before Hilliard returned, hurrying inside like he expected the house to be on fire.

"Everything okay?" Brian asked as he smoothly closed the front door.

Hilliard sighed. "Of course. I just have another load of things for the church sale." He seemed to be trying to keep himself busy as Brian worked his way through the rest of the repair items on the list. It only took a couple of hours to finish, and then he began packing up his tools to leave.

"I'm going to get the new water heater and the supplies for the steps. I'd suggest an on-demand one. It will provide more water and be more energy efficient. The unit will also take up less space in the utility room."

Hilliard seemed distracted but eventually nodded. "That sounds like a good idea."

Brian paused. "Is something wrong? Are you unhappy with some of my work?"

"Of course not." Hilliard smiled, but the warmth that had been there earlier had gone. "I'll see you tomorrow, and thank you for everything." Hilliard saw him to the door and closed it behind him.

Brian shook his head before making the run into Fort Bragg to get the supplies he needed, trying to put the weirdness out of his mind.

"How did it go?" his grandmother asked from her lift chair when he got home.

"Good, I guess. I got some repairs done and picked up the supplies for tomorrow," he explained, thankful his credit card had been able to stretch to cover it. He hated asking Gran for money to get him through. She'd give it to him—he knew she would help—but he didn't want to burden her with his problems.

"That's good. We got a few calls today, and I put the messages on your desk. Helen Russell wants you to put up a fence for her." She leaned forward. "What is it?"

"I don't know. Everything was great, and then he was gone for a while. When he came back, he was different and kept watching me like…. Shit…."

"Brian," Gran warned in the same tone she'd used when he was eight and said something bad.

"He went to the church."

Gran nodded. "I know. I already heard all about it. Ruth called me. It seems Violet had her gums flapping. Ruth said she cut her off and shamed her for gossiping, but she thinks Violet got Hilliard wondering."

Brian sat in one of the wingback chairs that had been in the same place in the living room for as long as he could remember. They were worn but warm and comfortable, like old friends. "What am I going to do? I suspect he'll probably cancel the work, as jittery as he seemed, and find someone else." At least he had the receipt for the supplies he'd bought and could return them, and he'd gotten some work.

Gran took his hands.

"Every time I think I'm about to get my feet under me and move on, something or someone decides that I'm not worth it, and I'm back in the crap hole again." He had spent three years trying to put his past behind him, and yet it came back to bite him all the time. "I work hard, Gran, and I never cheat anyone."

"I know, sweetheart," she said gently. "You've turned my house in a showplace, and I tell everyone that you did the work." Gran was the one person who had always been in his corner, believing him when no one else would.

"I know, but…." He could feel a good old-fashioned whine coming on, and he was not going to do that. There was nothing he could do to change what had happened. All he could do was try to move his life forward.

"You hold your head high and keep doing the work you do. Remember Helen…."

"She only hired me because the two of you are friends," Brian told her.

Gran squeezed his hands with her lotion-soft ones. If he closed his eyes, he could feel the comfort from those arthritic fingers seeping into him like always. "But you did good work, and now she calls you for help. You won her over and gained her trust." She released his hands and rested hers in her lap.

"But what do I do? I need the work, and I have all the supplies. What if he calls and cancels?" He hated worrying about shit all the time. He never used to do that, but now nervousness seemed to be his constant companion.

"Stop worrying. He hasn't called. Take the dogs out for a walk and try to clear your head. They need their exercise, and you need to get some fresh air and new perspective."

"Gran," he protested.

She sat back in the chair. "Look, I'm old, not all-seeing. I don't have all the answers. But take things as they come, and in the morning, go back and do your usual good job. That's what he wants—what all your clients want, in the end: a good job at a fair price. Everything else is just talk." That was his Gran, practical and down-to-earth. If she were younger, he swore she'd be out there helping him with the business. Gramps had run his own handyman business once he retired, doing jobs all over Mendocino County. As a teenager, Gramps had taken Brian out on jobs with him, and eventually he'd gone to work with him—until he passed away and everything in Brian's life went to hell. He stopped himself, because nothing good would come from going down that rabbit hole again.

"Are you hungry?" He got up.

"Walk the dogs first, please. I'm going to nap a little before dinner." She closed her eyes, and Brian got the leashes, sending Gigi and Poppy running around the room in excitement.

THE LITTLE hellions were surprisingly good for most of the walk, even prancing next to him, doing their best imitation of well-behaved dogs. Brian knew better and still had the scrapes to prove it. And as if to reinforce his opinion, as soon as they drew close to Hilliard's place, the two went nuts, barking and running in circles, nearly getting Brian tied up in their leashes again.

He looked toward the front door, but it stayed closed. Brian had hoped that maybe he would find Hilliard out and about and he could check if maybe he was seeing things that weren't there earlier. But the house was dark, and it looked like he wasn't home. The dogs peered through the gate slats, jumping and barking as though they could get Hilliard to come out and play.

"Come on, guys. Let's keep going," he said and tugged them forward.

"Brian?" Hilliard said as he came around the side of the house in jeans and an old red muscle shirt. He pulled out his earbuds. The dogs raced back, jumping, their tails wagging a mile a minute. "I see it's their walk time again." He smiled and went over to the gate. As soon as he opened it, the dogs ran over to him. Hilliard squatted down, his jeans pulling tight around his thighs. "Hey, guys. Are you being good and doing your best not to trip Brian?" he asked, handing out pets and scratches, both dogs wanting their turn for attention.

"They were good until I got close to the house. Then they went nuts." Brian couldn't help smiling at how they seemed to love Hilliard. In all the time he'd been walking them, they'd never reacted to this house at all, not until Hilliard moved in. "How is everything?"

"It's good. I got the trash hauled away and the donated items taken to the church. I feel like I can breathe in the house now. I was just working around the back, getting started on the yard and trying to figure out what constitutes a weed, but I gave up. Everything is so overgrown that I might start from scratch as far as the flowers go."

"Not a bad idea. She didn't have a lot in the yard, so you can pretty much do what you want without hurting anything."

Hilliard stood, his expression growing serious, and the dogs sat next to Brian, which was unusual. Maybe they sensed that something had changed. "Look, I need to ask you something…. One of the ladies at church said something, and…." He seemed uncomfortable, rubbing the back of his neck.

"I know. Ruth told Gran that one of the ladies was spreading gossip about the robbery at Violet Trainer's." He might as well rip off the Band-Aid and get this over with.

"It's really none of my business," Hilliard said gently, but there was tension in his eyes.

"But she got you wondering." Brian figured he should come clean.

Hilliard stood still and then nodded.

Brian came closer, and Hilliard opened the front door. Brian followed inside, the dogs happily coming along, jumping onto the sofa as if they owned the place.

"Can I get you something to drink?"

Brian shook his head. "I might as well get this done. See, I spent six months in jail. It was a one-to-two-year sentence, and I was released on parole after six months. Gran helped me get the business started, and I've been trying to rebuild my life since."

"What happened?" Hilliard asked matter-of-factly. Brian noticed that he didn't ask what he'd done. That was at least a hopeful sign that he wasn't going to get tossed out on his ear. "You don't have to tell me if you don't want to." He cleared his throat. "Back in Cleveland I was a lawyer, and I'm still deciding if I'm going to stay here or sell the house and return to Cleveland. If I stay, I'll apply to join the California bar."

"Okay," Brian said and took a minute to get his thoughts together. "One of the homes in town was broken into two and a half years ago. They stole a number of pieces of jewelry, silver, and some other small things that were easily traceable." His leg bounced on the floor. "I was with Gramps when it happened. He loved the coast, so he and I had been out driving and got home late." His throat ached as he thought about that day. "I'm glad we went, because Gramps went to bed that night and didn't wake up. It was heartbreaking for Gran and me, but he went happy, and the two of us had time with each other." He had to keep it together. "Two days after the funeral, I was accused of breaking into that house. They had found my fingerprints inside and got a warrant to search my residence and my truck, where they found one of the missing items. From there, I was guilty, even though I had been out with Gramps the entire day. He wasn't alive to testify, and they used that absence against me, turning the trip into me using my grandfather as a shield to steal. Gran testified, and they accused her of lying to cover for me. I never stole anything in my life. I was torn up about Gramps, and Gran was in pieces. She had lost her husband of nearly sixty years, and now I was accused of theft and eventually convicted."

"So they never found who actually committed the burglary," Hilliard supplied. "They looked at you, found what fit their narrative, and didn't look any further." He shook his head. "They had fingerprints and a stolen object in your vehicle, and downplayed any alibi that you had."

"That's pretty much it," Brian said. "I was convicted, and that was that. The case was closed, and they went on to other things." He was surprised that Hilliard seemed to believe him. No one else in town acted as if they did.

"If you didn't do it, then someone else did," Hilliard said. "And they got away with it. Do you have any idea who it was?"

Gigi jumped down and bounded into Hilliard's lap, while Poppy climbed into his. Brian petted the dog, happy for the comfort.

Brian shook his head. "It's a small town. I always thought that someone would open their mouth and say something they shouldn't, but nothing has happened other than the fact that everyone thinks it was me."

Hilliard sighed. "It must be hard making a living here with all that. Why didn't you move to Fort Bragg, or even down the coast toward the city? You could have found a lot of work there and pretty much left your past behind."

"I thought of that, but then I'd have to leave Gran. She can do some things but has arthritis really bad, so she is limited in what she can do for herself. I stay with her and look after her. She and Gramps were the only family I had left, and now it's just her. I can't leave her all alone, and I won't put her in a home. That would kill her. All her friends are here, and the church is here. So I stayed, and I'm doing the best I can." He found it hard to believe that Hilliard seemed to accept his story. So few people did.

"Well, it seems you have defenders. Ruth was definitely sticking up for you."

Brian leaned forward. "But why do you believe me? Most people don't."

Hilliard smiled. "In part because I had already figured out some of what happened. I'm a lawyer, and part of what I do is dig up information. It wasn't hard to find. The case seemed thin enough to me, especially given that the rest of the items have never turned up… just the one they found on you. Now why would you be dumb enough to leave something lying around to be found while being so good at hiding the rest that the police can't locate it?" Hilliard watched him like a hawk. "It doesn't make sense. Do you know if the police ever looked at your alibi, or did they simply discount it and go on?"

Brian shook his head. "I don't know what they did. The prosecuting attorney just went after me and Gran like we were members of some crime syndicate. She cried all the time, and they made me start to think that I might have done it." God, it had been so confusing. "In the end my attorney tried to get me a plea deal, but I was innocent and I wasn't going to say I did it, so…."

"They found you guilty, your attorney put in minimal effort, and you did six months for it."

Brian was speechless. "You actually believe me?"

Hilliard shrugged. "I have no reason not to believe you. It doesn't make any sense for you to make up a story like that. If you had broken into the house, you could simply have said that you made a mistake and that you were working to turn your life around or something. People make mistakes—God knows I have—but frankly, the details of your story are easy enough to check, so why bother to lie in the first place?" He sat back, and Gigi settled on his lap, soaking up the attention.

"Exactly. I suppose records of the burglary are public, and it's easy enough to verify the day Gramps died. As for the rest, I wish there had been a way for us to prove where we were. Gramps and I spent most of the day in the car. The coast around here is so rugged, and Gramps just wanted to drive and take in the scenery." God, they must have driven over two hundred miles that day. He would have been able to stand up for Brian and say where they had been, but with him gone, all the prosecutor had done was harp on the fact that Brian's alibi was a man who had passed away. "Anyway, I'm grateful." It was like a weight lifted off his shoulders.

"What, did you think I would fire you?" Hilliard asked. "Look, you showed up on time and did good work. What more could I ask?"

"Well, thank you." Brian felt better in some ways. "When I was first arrested, I told my story over and over and no one listened to me. Gran knew where I was that day, and she never doubted me." It had gotten him through those horrible six months of fear and worry that he had usually been able to keep out of his mind during the day, but otherwise….

Hilliard set Gigi gently on the floor, and she hurried over. Brian clipped on the leash and led the dogs out the front door. "I'll see you tomorrow." Brian smiled and waved before doing his best to lead the dogs down the walk back toward Gran's, already feeling lighter.

"You were gone a while," Gran said from in front of the television once he went inside. He unleashed the dogs, and they bounded right to Gran, one settling next to her and the other on her lap.

"He was nice," Brian explained.

Gran stilled. "You told him… everything?" She knew he never talked about it if he could help it. Those months were something he wanted to forget.

"I did, and he believed me. Hilliard is a lawyer, and he already knew part of the story. I think he looked me up on the internet. But he believed me." Though why he felt so inordinately happy puzzled him.

"He's a lawyer?" Gran asked. "Do you think if he believes you that he might think of a way to prove you didn't steal anything in the first place?"

Brian shrugged. That was almost too much to hope for.

Chapter 3

SOMETIMES IT seemed like nothing would go right. Hilliard was grungy and desperately needed a shower, but Brian was having trouble getting the new water heater installed. As of the last report, he thought he was getting close, which Hilliard hoped was the case. To prevent himself from hovering, he went upstairs to go through more of Aunt Grace's things and add more items to donate to the sale. He even managed to get his office set up, at least rudimentarily. With a place to sit and the window open, he logged on to his computer and accessed some of the legal websites he subscribed to.

It wasn't difficult to find information on Brian's case and even access the court records, since they had been digitized. The more he read, the more his blood boiled. Without thinking, he pulled over a pad and began making notes of items that seemed mishandled. It was fairly easy to see that Brian's defense had been minimal at best, and at worst, the lawyer was incompetent. Questions piled up as he read and wrote, but one thing was clear: Brian should definitely appeal his conviction. While Hilliard had wanted to believe Brian last night, everything he read now reinforced that he was right. Brian had been railroaded in a huge way, and he was still paying for it.

"Hill," Brian called up the stairs, "you have hot water."

Thank goodness. "That's great."

"I'm going to start on the steps," Brian said as Hilliard locked his computer out of habit and stood to head down the stairs. "They should take a few hours."

"Good. I was wondering if you could give me a quote for some additional work. I need the outside painted, and I need the wallpaper in the dining room stripped and the walls prepped for paint… along with the living room." The town had a lot of ordinances regarding the maintenance of properties in Mendocino, and he did not want to be ticketed or get on the bad side of any of the powers that be.

"I can do that," Brian said with a relieved smile. "Let me take some measurements when I'm done and I can work up an estimate. I have the equipment to spray the exterior, so that won't take long. What color were you thinking?"

"Aunt Grace painted the house butter yellow, and I like it, so I was thinking of keeping it the same color, just freshening it up." He snapped his fingers. "Also add a quote to paint the fence white." That should take care of the outside, especially once he got the garden under control.

Brian nodded and swallowed. "You know you don't have to do this because you're feeling sorry for me or anything." He wrung his hands. "I know what I told you last night, but you don't need to—"

Hilliard shook his head. "I don't. I have had lots of clients in my career. Some have been innocent, and others have been guilty as sin. I'm too jaded to do things like spend my money because I feel sorry for someone. I'm doing this because I need to get the house up to snuff, regardless of whether I stay, and you do good work." He knew himself well enough to be honest.

Brian looked beaten down for a second before his mask of civility fell back into place. "Well, okay, then. I'll put everything together tonight."

"Excellent. Maybe we can meet at the pub for breakfast to go over what you have, and then we can plan things going forward." He wasn't ready to tell Brian what he had found about his case. He wanted to see if he could get more information and develop a plan of his own, because as Brian had been convicted, it wasn't as simple as just poking holes. He needed to find solid evidence to present to the court and ideally figure out who had actually committed the crime. He also didn't want to give Brian hope if he couldn't deliver. The sadness that filled Brian's eyes when he thought Hilliard wasn't looking… it tugged at his heart. He wanted to do something about it, but he couldn't give Brian false hope.

"Okay. I can do that."

"Eight, then," Hilliard offered, and Brian agreed. "Then I'll let you get back to work." It seemed he had plenty more to do himself. House chores were not his favorite thing, but digging into a legal mystery? That really got his heart pumping. So once Brian left to get started, Hilliard put off his shower and practically bounded back upstairs to research procedures in California, as well as try to figure out what he would need to do to have a chance to overturn Brian's conviction.

HILLIARD YAWNED as he descended the sturdy new steps in front of the house. He strode toward the business portion of the village as he pulled on a sweatshirt to ward off the cool, damp air. Not much had changed since his visits years ago. The town still looked like something out of a different time. The homes all had a feel of having been there for decades, and some of the buildings looked like they would be more at home in a Maine whaling village than California. Aunt Grace used to tell him stories of when episodes of *Murder, She Wrote* were filmed in town. She had even gotten a part as an extra, so she always said she was also a resident of Cabot Cove.

Hilliard entered the pub and waited a few minutes for Brian before the hostess led them out to the covered patio area at the side of the building. "Did you walk down?" Brian asked. "The dogs saw me leaving and had a fit that I wasn't taking them along."

"I can just imagine." Brian looked amazing in tight chinos and a blue polo shirt that hugged his work-hardened chest. The man was a walking wet dream as far as Hilliard was concerned, and he lost his train of thought for a few seconds, simply staring at Brian like some sort of idiot.

"Yeah. They made such a ruckus that they woke Gran. I thought about bringing them with me, but I wasn't sure if you wanted to sit outside on a day like today," Brian went on, and thankfully Hilliard was able to pull his attention back where it should be.

"I like being outside and the fresh air. Even if the clouds are in and it's a little windy and damp." The marine layer had settled in thick over the town. "You could have brought the dogs. It would have been okay." He was coming to like them. They were loud sometimes, but that was because they were excited, and there were worse things than dogs being excited to see him. Hilliard picked up a menu from the center of the table. "I've never been here before."

"They have great omelets," Brian said and set down his menu. When the server returned, he ordered. Hilliard picked one with bacon and ham. "I thought I'd review the estimates. Painting the house is mostly some prep work, removing loose paint, and then taping off the windows and such. I can do that on a day when the sun is out and there isn't too much wind." He had an estimate that Hilliard found reasonable. "We can get the prep done ahead of time and then paint once the weather is right. I'll prep the steps at the same time. The fence is another issue. I'm going to need to replace some posts and crosspieces. There are places where the damp has gotten in. That will take some work, but then we can spray that as well and get it looking good."

He had estimates for all of it and had factored in Hilliard buying the paint. The wallpaper estimate surprised him. "What's this?"

"The wallpaper is from the fifties or sixties, and it's going to take time to get it off, wash down the walls of residual adhesive, and then sand and paint. This is a best guess. It could be more or less. And there is the possibility of asbestos in a house this old."

All the estimates seemed like they were possible. What Hilliard needed to do was take stock of his funds on hand and make some decisions about what he was going to do with his life. Going back to Cleveland was not particularly attractive. He would have money coming when his ex-asshole bought him out of their partnership, but he would need that to start up something new.

"Let's go ahead and start with the outside. Those tasks need to be done because they're visible. The painting inside we can see about once the rest is done." He initialed the estimates that he was ready to go ahead with. "Now, I have something else I need to speak with you about." He wasn't sure how to broach the subject, because while Brian had told him about his past, he hadn't gone any further. "I looked into what happened."

"I see," Brian said, and Hilliard wasn't sure if he was going to be angry or not.

"I told you I had already looked into your background. It's a lawyer thing. We see people with plenty of issues, legal and otherwise, so we become super anal about knowing who we're dealing with. Anyway… whoever handled your case did not do a good job. We could appeal the conviction on a number of grounds, including inadequate representation, but if you want, I think we should look at this from another point of view."

"That I'm out of prison and should just get on with my life," Brian said flatly.

If that was what he wanted, Hilliard would certainly keep out of it.

"That's what Gran told me. She says she knows I didn't do it and worries that if I stir it all up again, I'm only going to have a harder time." He sighed softly.

"You're welcome to do that and just move on. There is no shame in that sort of plan, and looking forward is always best. I tell my clients that all the time. But I believe you didn't do it, and the police simply looked no further once they had you in their sights."

Brian leaned closer. "What do you suggest?"

"Well, first, we follow some logic. If you didn't rob that house, then who did?" He held Brian's confused gaze. Digging into the case had answered some questions for him, including why Violet Trainer had acted the way she did. He was pretty sure she was the one who kept the town stirred up against Brian.

The server brought their food, but Brian didn't touch his. "Please eat," Hilliard said gently. He knew these sorts of sessions were stressful and that Brian was reliving a very painful time in his life. "How we go forward is up to you."

Brian sat still, and those huge eyes seemed to be searching for something. Hilliard felt their heat on him, but he refused to glance away. If Brian wanted his help, he'd be there for him. And if he wanted to walk away, then he'd abide by those wishes as well. "I don't know what to think. Maybe it's best to just let the past stay there."

Hilliard nodded. "Except is it really staying there?" he asked, and Brian shook his head.

"No. It seems to be all that anyone here talks about. Gran won't hear anything against me, and I love her for that, but…."

"You have other people in your corner. At least Ruth seemed to be," Hilliard said.

Brian half smiled and nodded. "She and Gran have been friends for years. When Gramps died and I was accused, Ruth stepped in to help Gran. While I was away, she was one who checked on Gran, and she even wrote me letters to let me know how Gran was doing." He swallowed hard, and Hilliard found himself aching to wipe that sadness off Brian's face. He seemed so beaten down, and Hilliard could tell he hadn't always been that way.

"The decision is yours," Hilliard said as he finally lowered his gaze and began eating the amazing breakfast. He refused to push Brian into anything, even though he was itching to get involved. It would give him something to sink his teeth into.

"Thanks," Brian said softly as Hilliard's phone dinged. He checked the message and cringed. "You okay?"

"My ex." Hilliard snatched up the phone and sent a reply to his message about a case they had been working on. He took a second and then replied with the answer, because he wasn't going to let Alan screw over the client. And then, to be a dick—but it felt good—he asked him where the money was from Alan's buyout of the firm. Then he muted the phone and set it screen down on the table so he wouldn't be tempted to look at the rant that was sure to follow. "He's a real ass."

His phone vibrated. Hilliard knew he shouldn't look, but he peered at the response. *Check your bank account.* Then the asshole sent a smiley face followed by a tombstone. Hilliard growled and knew he needed to take the same advice he gave his clients and let the past stay there, but he was still hurting—more than he wanted to admit to anyone, including himself. He ground his teeth, tempted to respond, but he shoved his phone in his pocket instead.

"I don't know what I ever saw in him," Hilliard muttered to himself, refusing to try to figure it out now. He had more important things to do than a postmortem on a disastrous relationship.

"Sorry," Brian said softly.

Hilliard shrugged. He had had plenty of difficult relationships, so why should he expect anything different from Alan? The truth was, he often wondered if he had some kind of loser magnet in his ass. He always seemed to attract one kind of guy. He thought Alan had been different, but nope. It had only taken a little longer for his inner loser to come out. "Thanks. I know I'm better off without him." He took another bite of his omelet and pasted on a smile. He didn't want his ex to ruin the morning.

"Did you come to visit a lot when you were a kid?" Brian asked.

Hilliard was grateful for the distraction. "A few times, mostly with my mom to see Aunt Grace. Dad usually had to work, and he'd stay in Cleveland while we came out here. The town hasn't changed very much, as far as I can see."

"What was your aunt like? I remember her as a nice lady."

"She was so cool. I remember her taking me to Glass Beach for sea glass and then taking me back to the house, where she showed me how to use the glass to make things. At the time, I made necklaces for some of my friends. When it wasn't foggy, she took me to the cliff so we could watch the sunset, and then as we walked through town, she told me stories about the people here. She showed me where Chinatown used to be and showed me pictures of the old windmills and stuff. One of her friends had one of the water towers on his property, and I got to climb up and look inside. It was empty, but I could see the entire town from up there." Some of the tension that he'd been carrying for weeks started to slip away. It was like walking down a happy, pleasant memory lane.

"Aunt Grace pointed out one of the buildings that she and the ladies at the historical society were trying to save from being torn down. They were really having a fight back then, and I told her when I grew up I'd be a lawyer and fight for people like her."

"What did she say to that?" Brian asked.

"Aunt Grace smiled and said she thought I'd be a good one. Then we climbed down and she took me to lunch." Hilliard sighed. "The thing is, I didn't even know that she remembered me. I hadn't seen her in quite a few years. I always figured that she would leave the house and stuff to my uncle. He's a much closer relative." Still, he was grateful to her every day.

"Sometimes we don't know what's going on in someone's mind. I get smiles from people all the time, and yet I know that behind my back, they're saying things about me and whispering." Brian sipped from his mug of coffee and set it down on the table. "I've really been trying to figure out why you've been so good to me. You didn't doubt me when others certainly have, and you've even offered to help me. I'm just not sure what I should do. Maybe it's best if I let sleeping dogs lie. At least that's where my head is right now."

"That's fine. You need to do whatever you feel is best for you."

"But I appreciate that fact that you care," Brian added.

Hilliard wanted to take his hand, but he wasn't sure if he should. Instead, he met those warm eyes with his gaze. Warmth raced through Hilliard. Something about Brian got his motor running, and it wasn't the fact that he had been treated badly. It wasn't pity. Hilliard liked to think that it was the fact that Brian had endured and found the inner strength to move on regardless of what people thought about him. And that was sexy as all hell, as far as he was concerned.

Chapter 4

BRIAN KNEW Hilliard was only trying to help him, but the more he thought about it, the more he knew that it was best if he didn't make waves. He was getting business, and people had short memories about some things. What he really wanted was to get on with his life and not look back. "I appreciate what you are trying to do." And the fact that Hilliard believed him meant more than he was willing to say. If he started down that road, he wouldn't be able to stop blathering. He was also worried that if he did try to clear his name and they failed, he'd be screwed. It would feel the same as being convicted and sentenced for something he didn't do all over again.

"I wanted to offer to help," Hilliard said as they finished their coffee. The server brought the check, and Hilliard paid the bill. "I'll meet you at the house." He smiled and hurried down to his car. Brian swore he could get addicted to that grin.

Brian made his way to the edge of the street where he had parked his truck.

"You should be ashamed of yourself."

The tone made him groan. He turned as Violet Trainer glared at him.

"You really should." She drew closer. "But what I want to know is where you hid the rest of what you stole."

"I never stole anything," Brian said, "and you need to get out of my way." He stepped to the side, and she did the same.

"I'm not afraid of you, and I know what you did." She glared as others on the sidewalk paused to watch.

Brian went around her and strode to his truck, his heart racing. He was tired of this kind of crap. When he reached his truck, he got in and backed out of his space. He headed out to Hilliard's, almost forgetting to come to a stop at one of the signs. When he arrived, he pulled up in front and climbed out, then knocked on the front door.

"What's up?" Hilliard asked.

"Let's do it. I want to find whoever committed the burglary, and so help me God, I want to clear my name. The pains in the asses here are not going to believe anything until I can prove I didn't steal anything."

Hilliard nodded. "I take it you ran into Violet."

"That woman is a—" Brian stopped himself from swearing. "How did you know?"

"I passed her in the car. She is never going to forgive and forget."

Not that Brian could blame her. It was her home that had been robbed, but he hadn't done it. "It's clear enough that no one is really going to change unless I can prove who really broke into that house. But I don't know where I should start. Detective stuff is not my strength, and I'm no Jessica Fletcher."

"O-kay," Hilliard said, rolling his eyes a little. "Well, the first thing is to request a copy of the court records. You can do that. They will make you pay a copying fee, but once we have that, we can see the case against you and try to tear it apart. I'll see if I can get a look at the police files. It isn't an active case, so I should be able to look at them. There could be some leads in there as well. They may have suppressed some real evidence—who knows? Reviewing old cases can be difficult, but we'll see what we can do."

"Thanks," Brian said softly. He had expended so much energy trying to fight what people thought. Two years out of jail and some days he was so tired of the fighting and working harder than everyone else just to make a living. Hilliard gently rested his hand on his shoulder, and Brian closed his eyes. It had been a long time since anyone had touched him in a caring way… well, anyone other than Gran.

Heat raced through him, and he was so tempted to close the gap between them. Hilliard was a stunningly handsome man, and Brian wanted nothing more than to discover what his full lips tasted like. Hell, he had lain awake at night wondering what Hilliard would feel like under him. But those were just fantasies, and he needed to keep his head in the real world. After a few seconds, Brian shifted his weight and forced his gaze away from Hilliard. It would be so easy to get lost in his eyes. His body ached in a way he hadn't known in a long time. That didn't change the fact that Hilliard was a client, and he needed to keep some sort of distance between them.

Still, that simple touch had been almost electric. Gran was gentle with him, but no one else was. In prison, he had been left alone. He was big enough to defend himself, and mostly he'd done his best to remain invisible. As a defense, it had worked, but had made for some very lonely months. Still, whatever he thought he felt changed nothing. He had to keep his head clear and act properly to keep some sort of professional standards.

"I should get to work," Brian said, his throat dry, and his voice sounded rough, even to himself. Besides, he needed a chance to think more clearly, and he couldn't do that with Hilliard near him. With a deep breath, he grabbed his tool belt and got to work.

"WHY ARE you smiling all the time?" Gran asked in that slightly nosy way of hers. "You were even whistling in the shower, and you haven't done that since…." She trailed off like she didn't want to say the words.

"Was I?" he asked as he strode to the kitchen to make them some dinner. He had the things for a salad, and Gran liked his pesto, so he started the pasta water.

"Yes, you were." Gran slowly made her way over, using her cane for balance. Brian was tempted to help her, but instead he just continued watching her in case she needed help as he tore the lettuce. Gran sat in the chair at the small kitchen table. "And don't think you can just leave the room when you don't want to talk about something. I may be an old lady, but I can still get around. Now what's going on?"

"You sound like I did something bad," Brian said.

"Piff. I like that you're happy, and I'm thinking it has to do with that new client of yours." Gran might nap more than she used to and have trouble walking, but she didn't miss anything. "Is he hot?"

"Gran…." Brian set the knife he'd grabbed to cut cucumbers on the cutting board.

She rolled her eyes. "The younger generation didn't invent hotness, you know. Your grandfather was scorching when I first met him. He worked in one of the mills and had muscles for days. He also had a fancy car, and all the girls had their eye on him, but I was the one he chose. And let me tell you, he turned out to be even hotter between the sheets than he was on the beach." She practically cackled as Brian groaned and turned away. The last thing he wanted to hear was that Gramps had been a stud. "You know that kept him alive for years."

"I'm trying to make dinner, and I'm going to cut a finger off." He could barely see straight, his eyes were watering so badly from a mixture of laughter and sadness. Brian wiped his eyes and set the knife down. "I'll bite—how did being a stud keep Gramps from dying, considering he had a heart attack four years ago?" He knew he was going to regret this, but sometimes he had to just let Gran get her story out.

"Ten years ago, the doctors said that he needed to get more exercise, so we started taking walks through town, going to classes in Fort Bragg at the community center… and at night… let's just say that passion is a great way to burn the calories. I swear that kept him around for the next six years."

He picked up the knife and shook his head. "Sex kept Gramps alive all that time."

"Yup. I'm just that good." She held out her hand and did a mic drop. Brian had no idea what he was going to do with her, but he finished the salad without cutting himself—or looking at Gran, for fear she'd start another story. One scandalization was enough for the evening. "And I want you to have that." Great, they were back to him.

"I'm fine, and please don't get involved. Hilliard is a nice man, and he's going to help me prove I'm innocent. He's also a client, and I can't go around getting involved with the people I work for." He finished with the salad and divided it between two bowls before adding the pasta to the boiling water.

"Yeah, but he also makes you whistle and smile." She was such a pill.

"How do you know that I'm not happy just being here with you?" he countered.

Gran smiled and got out of her chair to pat his cheek from across the prep table. "Because I know you, and I like seeing you happy. Besides, that kind of happiness comes from meeting someone you like. You aren't going to work for Hilliard forever, and as long as the two of you aren't getting busy during work hours, there really isn't an issue." She sat back down, leaning slightly on her cane.

"Gran, don't be pushy," he said gently. "I'm happy, okay? I'll admit that. And I like Hilliard. He's attractive and smart—way smarter than me." He got out the pesto from the refrigerator and then checked on the pasta.

"Maybe you should invite him here for dinner. I'll make some of my special light-as-air fried chicken. Your grandfather used to say it was the best of the best and why he fell in love with me." A faraway smile settled over her face. "He always said that I was beautiful, and when he found out I could cook… he knew he was a goner." She sighed softly. "I really miss him."

Brian stopped what he was doing and hurried to her. "Are you okay?"

"Of course. Sometimes it sucks being alone, and I don't want that for you." That plaintive expression was too much for him, and he felt his resolve melting like an ice cube in July.

"Okay, Gran. I'll invite him to dinner. He said there would be things I needed to sign so he could get copies of the records and stuff. I'll invite him over so we can get that done and you can meet him, but after that, you need to promise me that you won't meddle."

"Me?" She straightened up, her eyes big. "I never meddle, and shame on you for saying so. I push a little and *plutz* sometimes." Whatever that meant. "But I never meddle. Now Violet, she meddles in everything, and I will not have you comparing me to that woman."

He returned to making dinner. "I think you got yourself a little off track." Sometimes he wondered if she was slipping a little, though this was not one of them.

BRIAN SPENT the rest of the evening with Gran, and the following day, as he prepped the house for painting, he managed to get a few minutes with Hilliard. Judging by the bags of trash he was hauling out to the new Mustang convertible that the transport company had delivered just the day before, and filling the back seat, Hilliard was still cleaning out the house.

"The weather is supposed to be good tomorrow, with minimal fog," Brian said once he had the plastic up over the last window. He had been working to make sure he had the place ready for the next sunny day. With the town right on the coast, those could be scarce as hen's teeth.

"Great. Are you going to need help? I've been tackling Aunt Grace's project-slash-junk room, and…." He shook his head and set yet another bag of trash near his car.

"I think so. It's a big job, but it should go fast with the sprayer and the fact that we're not changing the color." He climbed down off the ladder. "If you want, you can put those bags in the back of my truck, and I'll take them to the dump when I'm done for the day."

"Thank you," Hilliard said, and Brian got a smile that set his heart beating a little faster. God, he was being so stupid. A simple smile and he was over the moon. Part of him felt like a swooning teenager, and he was way past that age. Heck, he didn't even know if Hilliard might be interested, but judging by the way he seemed to lose his train of thought around Brian every now and then, it was a possibility. Not that Brian could act on anything between them. Still, Hilliard had an amazing smile, just quirked enough that Brian had to admit it made the man hot as all hell, especially today, in a T-shirt a size too small that hugged his lithe body like a second skin.

"Oh, Gran asked me to invite you to dinner. Apparently she is going to make her famous chicken." God, he could have issued the invitation a hell of a lot more smoothly than that. "Believe me, it's something else. She's planning to make it tomorrow, so…." He shifted his weight nervously.

"That sounds wonderful," Hilliard said. "I'd love to meet your grandmother." They both stood still, like they each wanted to say something but neither of them dared to. Brian wished he had the guts to tell Hilliard that he liked him. The words were on the tip of his tongue, but he reminded himself that getting involved personally with Hilliard was a bad idea, even as he felt an unstoppable pull toward the other man. Hilliard even leaned closer, his lips parted slightly, and Brian was so tempted to see what they tasted like.

"Morning," someone called from the road as they walked their dog. Hilliard blinked before standing up straighter, while Brian adjusted the ladder for something to do, relieved that fate, and a small dog stopping to do its business, had taken the decision out of his hands.

Hilliard waved and knelt down, and the small poodle mix wagged her tail madly as she hurried over for pets. "How is Lucy this morning?" Hilliard asked as he petted the exuberant dog.

"Much better," the man said. Hilliard stood, and the man nodded to Hilliard, and then both man and dog continued down the road. Clearly Hilliard might be new in town, but he was already making friends. That was good, because Brian was hoping that Hilliard would decide to stay, though nothing more had been said about his plans.

"Mr. Stevenson walks his dog every afternoon," Hilliard explained. "Lucy was dragging a few days ago, but she seems better now." He sighed. "Well, I had better get these bags loaded or else I'm never going to get this done."

Brian turned away as a group of teenagers on bikes came down the street, pedaling to beat the band. As they passed Hilliard's car, one of them reached out and grabbed one of the plastic bags. It ripped and he continued on, the black plastic flapping behind him, spilling the contents of the bag all over the inside of the car.

"Jackasses!" Brian called as Hilliard groaned.

"Who the hell was that?" Hilliard asked, hands on his hips as he surveyed the mess his car had become.

"The fucktard four," Brian snapped. "Kendall and Kevin, Violet's grandsons, and their partners in crime, Nathan West and Michael Rogers. You'd think they were still twelve." He went inside and grabbed a fresh bag to help Hilliard clean up the mess. Then Brian set about transferring the rest of the black bags to the back of his truck, and he returned to the ladder to finish his prep, glancing at Hilliard every few minutes because he just couldn't help himself.

"Did you ask him?" Gran said as soon as he walked in the house. Sometimes she was just too much.

"Yes. I'm painting his place tomorrow, and he's going to help me, so I figured the least I could do was offer him some dinner." He was not going to tell Gran anything more than that. His growing wonder about his client was not something she needed to know. Besides, the more he thought about it, the more he was convinced that he was just seeing things the way he wanted to as opposed to how they really were. After all, Hilliard was a successful, handsome man with everything going for him, and Brian was an ex-con trying to find a way to make a living. There were tons of people that Hilliard could choose over him.

"Is that the reason you told him or the excuse you're telling yourself?" Sometimes Gran was too observant for her own good. "You can't pull the wool over my eyes. And in case you're wondering, you're as good as anyone else. You didn't do what you were accused of, so don't let yourself act as if you aren't."

Sometimes she knew just what to say. "Thanks, Gran."

"Now go on up and get cleaned up." She flashed him a gentle smile. "And don't forget to whistle or sing—whatever makes you happy." She took his hand. "Remember that it doesn't matter what anyone in this damned town says. You and I know the truth. You were with Gramps when that burglary took place. I know it, and so do you. So don't you dare give anyone, including the big-mouth gossips, any mind at all." He could always count on Gran to be in his corner no matter what.

Chapter 5

Somehow Hilliard ended up covered in paint. It wasn't as though Brian actually tried to spray him; Hilliard just seemed to be a magnet for every stray bit of the stuff. His old jeans and navy T-shirt were spattered with butter-colored splotches that resembled stars if he looked at them a little off-focus. His hair and skin were covered with flecks of the stuff too. "You even managed to get some on your nose," Brian teased, because his own clothes and skin were nearly pristine. How in the laws of physics they managed that was beyond Hilliard's understanding. Maybe Brian was coated in Teflon and the shit just bounced off of him and onto Hilliard.

Brian returned to the last section of house and applied an even layer of paint, the gun hissing and the compressor kicking in, covering up the ever-present roll of the ocean just below the cliffs at the edges of town.

"Is that it?" Hilliard asked as he stepped back from the ladder he'd been holding steady. Part of the yard was just uneven enough that he figured it was safer than letting Brian go up on his own. Besides, with Brian on the ladder and Hilliard holding it, he got to watch Brian, and that provided one hell of a view—even better than the rocks with waves crashing over them in the cove a few streets over. The man had an ass to die for, that was for sure, and the way he was standing only accentuated the way his back curved and then flowed into a perfect bubble butt.

"It looks like it," Brian said, checking out his work before climbing down. "We just need it to dry. Thankfully the breeze is slight today and the sun warm enough that it shouldn't take long."

"That's great." Hilliard stepped back to take in the entire house and smiled. It did look good, and with some touch-ups on the trim once the main walls were dry, the old house would look like she should once again. Now all they needed to do was paint the fence, and then he could replace the roses that grew on the arbor over the front gate and the place would be just as he remembered from his visits years ago. He just had to figure out how he was going to tackle the inside, since his budget would only go so far. The money Alan wired him from the practice needed to stay in the bank. That was his capital—money he'd need to either buy into a new firm in Cleveland or start a practice in town. He still wasn't sure what he wanted to do. "I really love how it looks."

"Good. I want to wait an hour or so before taking down the plastic." He started cleaning the paint sprayer using a bucket and the hose, letting the pieces soak as he closed up the ladder before loading it onto his truck rack.

While Brian packed up the rest of his equipment, Hilliard went inside, not daring to touch anything except the door to the old refrigerator until he got out of his clothes and into the shower. He grabbed a couple bottles of water and took one out to Brian, who had started removing the plastic from the side of the house he'd painted first.

"Thank you." Brian twisted off the lid and drank half the bottle, with a small drip of water running down his chin that Hilliard wanted desperately to lick off that tempting sun-bronzed skin. "I needed that." He licked his lips, and Hilliard nearly dropped his water bottle.

"No problem." Hilliard stepped out of the way so Brian could finish his work. As much as he wanted to stay here and watch Brian, he went inside and right into the bathroom.

Stripping off his clothes, he sighed and willed himself not to think of Brian, but it was impossible. By the time he stepped under the hot water, his cock pointed north. At first he tried to ignore it, but when he closed his eyes, he could almost feel Brian in there with him, his rough hands running over Hilliard's chest and down his belly before callused fingers wrapped around his cock, tugging just the way he liked. Damn, that felt good. He moaned softly, reaching for the soap. He slicked his hand, still imagining Brian's, and slowly stroked himself, the water running over him, heating his skin, adding to the sensation, which grew more intense with each stroke. Fuck, he could almost feel Brian right behind him, his chest pressed to Hilliard's back, the impressive cock he'd caught hints of in his work clothes pressed to Hilliard's ass, strong arms holding him upright as he continued stroking, sending Hilliard flying on wings of delight until he could take it no more. His leg bounced as pressure built inside until his breath hitched and he tumbled into sweet release.

The water continued flowing over him as Hilliard breathed deeply, letting his mind return to the present. Then, with a soft sigh, he returned to his lonely reality. Hilliard grabbed the soap and began the mundane task of scrubbing off all the damned paint, leaving his skin red when he was done.

Once he was showered and dried, he wrapped the towel around his waist and checked out front. Brian was just loading up two black trash bags before climbing into the truck. Hilliard stepped away from the window so Brian wouldn't see him watching and went to the closet and looked through the hangers to try to figure out what to wear.

HILLIARD WOULD never tell anyone, but it took three outfit changes before he looked the way he thought he should. He wanted to look good, but he didn't want to seem like he was trying too hard. He wasn't sure if this was a date, a meet-my-family sort of thing. More likely it was just dinner. He didn't want to seem like a schlub either way, but he didn't want to dress like he was going on a date, because what if Brian didn't feel that way? And who had a dinner date with their grandmother there? Hilliard was going in circles and needed to stop his mind from short-circuiting completely. In the end he settled for tan slacks and a blue-, green-, and white-striped polo shirt.

Brian had given him the address, so he walked the three blocks toward the ocean and one block over to the obviously well-cared-for light green house with white trim. The garden was immaculate, filled with flowers in an array of colors that took his breath away. As he approached the door, the dogs went nuts inside, and Brian appeared. For a second he wondered if Brian had been watching for him.

"Knock it off. You know him. He isn't here to eat you." Brian opened the screen door, and both dogs hurried out, barking until he knelt down. Then they went nuts, winding around him in a dance for attention. They practically jumped over each other to get to him, and Hilliard made sure to pet them both. "Let him come inside," Brian said, and he stood, the dogs hurrying back through the door. Hilliard followed, handing Brian the bottle of wine he'd had in the house. He hoped it was good.

"Thanks for having me over. I was starting to get tired of my own cooking." He smiled as Brian closed the door after him, and got a whiff of his earthy scent as he passed by. "Cleveland is many things, but there's a vibrant restaurant scene."

"There are a few decent restaurants in town and some more in the area, but you have to pick and choose. The Mack House here in town is good—"

"Especially their chicken, but it doesn't hold a candle to mine." A frail-looking woman came into the room and stopped to hold the door frame. "But then, not much does."

"Gran, if this is too much…," Brian said.

"Nonsense." She smiled and instantly seemed much younger. "I don't get to cook much, and I needed to pass on my secret to someone before I check out for the last time." She made her way up to Hilliard. "I'm Beverly, and you must be Hilliard. I've already heard things about you." She looked him over. "Ruth was right—you are hunky."

Hilliard blushed. "Thank you?"

Beverly waved her hand. "Don't play humble with me. You know you turn heads. Heck, if I were a few decades younger…."

"Well that's sweet of you, but I tend to flow in a different direction. Still, I bet you turned heads too."

"Enough of your sweet talk." Beverly sat down in what Hilliard assumed was her chair.

"Gran, what about the rest of dinner?" Brian hurried into the kitchen. Hilliard figured he needed to stay out of his way.

"Everything is fine," Beverly said, but Brian seemed to have a different opinion as he checked the things on the stove, turning down burners as well as the oven.

"No, it wasn't," he said gently before returning to the living room. "All the burners were on full, and everything would have scorched." He sat next to her.

"I finished the chicken," Beverly said with much less force than she had before. Brian patted her hand and nodded as the last of her energy seemed to leave her and she closed her eyes. Brian grabbed a blanket that rested on the arm of the sofa and spread it over her. Then he tilted his head toward the kitchen, and Hilliard joined him, with the dogs following, their nails clicking on the floor.

"I'm sorry. I should have known this would be too much for her." Brian opened the refrigerator and handed Hilliard a beer before checking on dinner once more. "She got everything together, but I think standing at the stove wore her out."

"Will she be okay?" Hilliard asked, his gaze going to where she rested.

"Yes. Gran catnaps a lot. Dinner is going to be a few minutes yet, so I'll just let her rest. She was determined to make dinner herself." He lowered his gaze, and Hilliard tried to figure out why. "She appreciates that you're helping me." He leaned closer. "And I think this is Gran's way of feeling you out."

"Huh?" Hilliard said. "I don't get it."

Brian hesitated, and Hilliard knew from his legal training that it was best just to give people time and not push them to talk to you. Brian grew more nervous by the second and then shook his head. "This is probably a really bad idea."

Hilliard could feel Brian pulling away, locking whatever he wanted to say back behind the walls he had put up in order to protect himself. Not that Hilliard blamed him. If he had been through what Brian had, he'd have walls the size of Everest. "What?" he asked softly. "You're leaving me a little in the dark here."

"He means that I'm a pushy old broad," Beverly said from the other room, not sounding the least bit tired. "And that I wanted to invite you over to see if you were interested in my grandson." Clearly someone had been playing their own version of possum.

"I see." He turned back to Brian. "Why didn't you just ask?"

Brian rolled his eyes. "How exactly do I phrase that question? You're a lawyer, and I'm an ex-con hoping to clear his name. So do I say something like, 'Hey, I think you're handsome, but I've been to prison for burglary. You wanna get busy or something?'"

Hilliard snorted. "Did anyone ever tell you that you're kind of bad at this sort of thing? How about something like…." He set his beer on the counter and moved closer to Brian, watching him swallow but feeling the heat build between them the closer he got. He looked into Brian's eyes. "I think you're hot and thought you might feel the same way about me. So if you're inclined, maybe we could have dinner and go to a movie or something."

Brian snorted. "Are we teenagers now?"

Hilliard shrugged. "All my past relationships started out hot, and look how they turned out. The last one crashed and burned when I found out Alan was screwing every younger guy he could get to bend over his damned desk." He took a deep breath to try to calm himself down. Brian stepped back as Hilliard felt the anger washing off himself. It was not a good feeling. "I think I need a chance to get over him."

"I see." Brian turned back to the stove. "I understand that. Not everyone is ready to date or that sort of thing. We can keep our dealings professional. That's perfectly fair."

"Oh poo," Beverly said from the other room. "Hilliard is saying he needs to take things slow, not push you away. God, sometimes you men don't know how to communicate for crap."

"That's enough from the peanut gallery in there," Brian snapped without any heat. "You were the one who was supposed to be making dinner, you know." He took pots off the stove and began mashing potatoes and putting butter on veggies.

"Maybe, but your gran is right. We don't need to rush into things. I have a lot of the mess from Alan to clean up. He might have bought me out of the practice, but I still need to figure out what I am going to do professionally, and I think I need to get to a place where I don't want to wring the bastard's neck every time I mention his name." Apparently he had a lot of unresolved anger and resentment issues that he needed to figure out.

"I'm usually right," she added, and Brian rolled his eyes as he got out bowls and began getting the food ready to serve. "I'd like a beer with dinner."

"You know what the doctor told you," Brian said.

The most undignified sound came from the living room, and Hilliard smiled. "She's something else."

"Try living with her," Brian retorted with a gentle smile.

"I'm over eighty, and one beer is not going to kill me. And if it does, then I'm a lot closer to the jumping-off place than I think I am." She pushed off the blanket and got up out of her chair, grabbed her cane, and headed slowly to the table. Hilliard helped Brian bring in the food, with Brian placing a glass of beer at Beverly's place. Then they all sat down to what looked like the best home-cooked meal he'd had in years.

"So how do you propose to help prove that Brian didn't rob anyone?" Beverly asked over a piece of her to-die-for cherry cobbler.

"I'm not sure. The easiest way would be to try to verify his alibi. I'm assuming the police tried to do that when the case was first investigated."

Beverly snorted. "This place may look like Cabot Cove, but there most definitely is no Jessica Fletcher in this town. Heck, as far as the police are concerned, it's more like Mayberry and all the cops are Barney Fife. They saw what they wanted to see and then didn't go any further. They figured they had enough evidence and that was that."

Hilliard looked to Brian. "If that's the case, then I think we need to recreate the road trip you and your grandfather took. See if there aren't cameras, receipts, someone who remembers the two of you. Anything to help us prove your story."

Brian shook his head and shrugged. "He and I went up and down the coast. It was just a road trip where we stopped at anything that caught our fancy."

"Then we'll divide it up. Go north one day and then south another. If there is a way to provide you with an alibi, then it will be out there somewhere. I'd also like to look into who might have really perpetrated the burglary. We all believe that it wasn't Brian, so that means it was someone else, and we can assume it wasn't some random stranger, because they would not have the knowledge to try to pin it on Brian. This was someone from town, someone who knew Brian was away." He leaned over the table. "Someone close enough to be aware of what was happening in your lives."

"Great," Beverly said. "Now we need to be looking at all our friends."

"Or enemies," Hilliard supplied. "Who would have access to the burglary site? Who knew what was there?"

Gran sipped her beer. "That's easy. Any of the family. Violet comes from a bunch of money-grubbers. They would all sell each other out for a dime if they thought they could get away with it." She took a moment to think. "That year the historical society did one of their fundraisers. Violet and a number of others opened their homes for historical house tours. They sold tickets and everything."

Hilliard groaned. "So any one of the people who came through could have seen what she had and returned to rob the place." Great. That meant their chances of finding the thief were between zero and nothing.

"Gran, Violet would have put away anything she didn't want people to see. We went on that tour, and the house looked bare, remember? You remarked that Violet seemed to have stripped the house to the walls, which you thought was an improvement because her place was usually cluttered to the gills."

"Okay, let's look past the home tour, because that isn't going to get us anywhere. It is possible that someone may have scoped out the house at that time, but why only that one? There were others on the tour, I'm sure. Why was only that house targeted, especially if all the valuables had been put away?" He was pretty sure the house tour had little bearing on the burglary. "It's likely the thief was closer to home."

"But how do we figure it out?" Beverly asked.

"That's pretty easy. We need to talk to the people involved. Get closer and see what we can find out. Do you think you can arrange it so we can talk to Violet? I'd like to get a look inside the house and maybe see where the things that had been stolen were kept."

"I don't know. Violet loves to have people over. She thinks of herself as the queen of the town. Nothing happens here without her knowing about it, and she loves to talk, but maybe not to me. Before all this business, she used to call every now and then, and I was lucky if I could get her off the phone after an hour. We'll have to see on that front."

"Okay. You work that angle, and maybe on Saturday, Brian and I can take a road trip and see what we can find out." He ate the last bite of his cobbler and sat back in the chair. It had been a long time since he'd had a meal like that, and it had been amazing.

Brian began clearing the table, and Hilliard got up to help carry the plates and things to the sink. "You don't need to do that."

Hilliard finished helping Brian clear the table while Beverly settled in her chair with the dogs curled at her feet. "I should get going, but thank you for dinner. It was bellisima."

"You're welcome," Beverly said from her chair, and Hilliard took her hand. She smiled at him. "Come over any time. Brian is a really good cook." Was this one of those "let the matchmaking begin" kinds of situations? He wasn't sure.

Brian walked Hilliard outside and down to the front gate, then opened it for him. "I'm glad you could come, and I really appreciate you helping me. I had no idea where to start, and it sounds like you have a plan."

"Of sorts. I don't know if anything is going to come of it, but we can at least try." Hilliard was about to turn to leave, but he paused, meeting Brian's gaze once more, and this time, he let the heat and longing in those eyes pull him closer. Without thinking, he gently cupped Brian's cheeks and kissed him. He had intended on a gentle, soft kiss, but within seconds the fire between them flamed to life and Hilliard deepened the kiss, unable to stop himself and not wanting to.

Brian was delectable, and Hilliard could feast on those lips for hours, but he was finding out that in addition to being a town of water towers, Mendocino also had its share of gossips, and he wasn't going to give them fodder, for both his and Brian's sakes. "I'll see you tomorrow." His throat was dry and the words sounded rough, but he got them out and then turned and headed away from the Pacific, closer to the center of town. Hilliard couldn't help turning back to smile and wave at Brian as the evening marine layer rolled in.

Chapter 6

BRIAN LAY awake, staring at the ceiling, replaying the kiss on an endless loop. He blinked as the door slowly opened and the dogs jumped onto the bed and settled on either side of him. Damn, who would have thought a single kiss could get him so wound up? And yet it was the middle of the night and it was all he could think about.

"You guys like Hilliard," he said. Both dogs lifted their heads in a *Why are you talking now?* kind of look. "I know. You like anyone who is willing to scratch your head and give belly rubs."

Gigi blinked at him and then put her head down once more. He knew he was being stupid and just needed to settle down. The dogs drew closer as the evening air chilled the room. He liked to sleep with a window open to catch the fresh air and so he could hear the waves as they crashed against the coast.

Footsteps in the hall drew his attention, and he got up to find Gran using her walker to get to the bathroom. "Why are you still up?"

"Can't sleep," Brian said.

"I can't either, but I'm old. What's your excuse?" she retorted, and Brian rolled his eyes. "Does it have to do with our dinner guest?"

"Gran," he said softly.

"I saw you two, and I saw the way he kissed you. It was damned steamy, and now you're up in the middle of the night. It sounds to me as though you have Hilliard on your mind." She continued on, and Brian went back to his room. The dogs had moved to where he'd been sleeping, taking up the warm spot on the bed. Brian scooted them over and climbed back under the covers, hoping he might be able to rest. Fortunately, once Gran had returned to her room, he rolled over and sleep finally came to him.

Still, he dreamed of a dark-haired man with intense eyes who kissed him like the world was ending. Those strong arms held him tight, and he wanted more, but the man stayed just far enough away that Brian couldn't draw him closer, no matter what he did or how much he wanted to. The kisses were intense, but he couldn't seem to touch him.

The dogs whimpered when he sat straight up in bed, breathing deeply, hard as a rock and wondering what the hell was going on. Both dogs blinked at him and then jumped down from the bed, probably going to sleep with Gran because she didn't thrash around. Brian needed to rest—he had work to do today—but his subconscious had other ideas. Still, he lay back down, hoping his mind would quiet.

BRIAN YAWNED as he touched up the trim on Hilliard's house. He held the brush still as the uncontrollable motion went through him.

"It looks almost done," Hilliard said from behind him.

Brian didn't dare turn around. He wanted to, but every time he saw Hilliard, his mind made these flights of erotic fantasy that he needed to keep under control. It had only been a kiss, but his mind was charging ahead full speed. "It is." He continued with the last of the touch-ups and then climbed down from the ladder. "I got some floor paint for the treads on the new stairs, but I think we need to wait a while for the wood to age before we paint it. I just have the fence repairs to go." He needed to keep things professional since he was working.

"That's good. And I have to figure out what I'm going to do with this yard. Everything is overgrown and out of control." Hilliard had already pulled out a lot of weeds and had most of the beds cleared, but now they were empty patches of earth. "I suppose that can wait until we finish up the other work."

Brian felt Hilliard's gaze on him as he set down the brush. "The garden center here offers design work. You might want to get them to make up a plan for you, and then all you'd have to do is plant what they suggest. Gardening isn't one of my areas of expertise, but they've helped a number of the inns and other people in town." He dared a glance at Hilliard and found him smiling at him. Damned if Brian didn't grin back like an idiot. He stepped toward Hilliard and looked at the house.

"Wow, what a difference. This looks so much better."

"It does." Brian lifted his gaze upward as the fog thickened. Just an hour ago, the sky had been clear, but now the haze and clouds obscured the sky, lying low over the land. Fortunately most of the painting was done, with only the touch-ups still wet. The weather was highly unpredictable, and sometimes you just had to go with whatever happened.

"Are we still on for tomorrow?" Hilliard asked. "I thought we could meet here about nine and go south."

Brian nodded. "That would be good. But I hope I'm not causing you a whole bunch of trouble."

"Where did that come from?" Hilliard asked. He seemed to be holding his breath.

Brian suddenly felt exposed. He wished he hadn't said anything, but he had already opened the can of worms. "Sometimes I think I'm the one person who is destined to be a pain in the ass for everyone else. I can't seem to just go through life unscathed. Gran has had to put up with a lot, and now I'm foisting my problems onto you. I just think that maybe everyone would be better off is I wasn't around."

"That's bullshit. Your grandmother stuck around because she loves you, and I may not be a trained investigator, but I'm going into this with my eyes open. I know what I'm doing, and I agreed to help you." Hilliard lightly touched his shoulder. "You don't need to second-guess yourself all the time."

"I guess," Brian whispered. It would be nice to have proof that he hadn't carried out the burglary. He knew he had been with Gramps at the time, and he had never stolen from anyone. But that didn't seem to matter to a lot of folks in town. "Guilt or innocence doesn't seem to make a difference to anyone once you've been to jail. As far as most people are concerned, I did it, and they won't look beyond that."

"Well, what we have to do is prove that you didn't. Once we do that, everyone is going to know you were wrongly convicted. So we take a road trip tomorrow and try to find someone who remembers seeing you and your grandfather that day. We'll also look into who actually did the burglary. They can't hide forever. Someone knows more than they're saying. We simply need to get to the bottom of what happened." He squeezed lightly, and Brian closed his eyes, his entire being concentrating on that one point where Hilliard touched him.

"But what if we do this and no one cares?" That was his true worry. All that everyone would remember was what he was accused of.

Hilliard chuckled. "In a town this size, everyone is going to know what happened. And once they do, things will change." He squeezed once more, and then his hand fell away. "Just relax, and let's concentrate on finding the proof we need. From there, we can appeal your conviction on the grounds of new evidence that proves it couldn't have been you."

Brian turned to Hilliard. He seemed so confident that Brian wanted badly to believe him. But he had already seen that the justice system didn't always get it right. And what if they had the proof and no one cared anyway?

No, he had to put that aside and let Hilliard do what he did best. At some point he had to trust someone.

"Okay. I'll be here tomorrow at nine, and we can look for a needle in a haystack." He just hoped that the needle was actually there to be found.

"READY?" HILLIARD asked as Brian approached the house. The clouds hung over the coast, and there was even a bit of mist in the air.

"As I'll ever be." Brian wasn't convinced that this would do any good. After all, it had been over two years. People changed jobs, and it wasn't likely anyone was going to remember him and Gramps. Still, if Hilliard wanted to spend his time doing this, who was he to tell him no?

"Then let's get to it." Hilliard led the way around to the side and unlocked the Mustang. He slid in and started the engine. Then he pressed a button and the roof slid back. "We might as well have some fun while we tool down the coast."

That grin was infectious, and for a second Brian forgot why they were going. He climbed in, and Hilliard pulled out to drive through town. It took about two minutes before the wind in Brian's hair blew out some of the old cobwebs he hadn't realized were there. By the time they turned onto the main road heading south, Brian had his eyes closed and let the wind carry him away.

"There's really something amazing about the convertible, and it isn't the sun, but the wind and the air. I have a few sweatshirts in back if it gets chilly, but I love having the top down."

"Me too. I think this could become my favorite car thing."

Hilliard laughed. "What's your current favorite?"

Brian chuckled. "Maybe connecting the car to my phone so I can choose my own music." He smiled as Hilliard handed him a cord and told him to go for it. Soon enough, they had added a soundtrack of '80s dance tunes to their drive. Brian didn't know if this could get any better, but by the time they crossed the Little River bridge, they were singing along, and Brian actually thought this could be a day to remember.

The song changed, and Hilliard laughed. "Oh my God, ABBA?" he cried, and before long the two of them were singing to "Dancing Queen" at the top of their lungs. The fun continued into Queen's "We Will Rock You" and "We Are the Champions" until they were both grinning like fools, singing until they were nearly hoarse.

They drove around a bend in the road, and Brian stopped singing.

"That's the Point Arena Lighthouse. Gramps and I stopped there to see the light and the sea lions. The turnoff is a mile or so up ahead."

And just like that, the reason they were here came rolling back over them. Hilliard made the turn, and they continued out along the point toward the ocean, the white light tower growing closer and more impressive as they drew near.

"Gramps always loved it here. The light itself is okay." Brian motioned, and Hilliard pulled over. "It's the seals and sea lions that are the real stars here."

"I get that. But we need to see if anyone can help place you here that day. What would be memorable about you and him?"

Brian paused because he hadn't really thought about how this would work. "Gramps had this real thing about lighthouses, and apparently he'd been reading, so he probably had a conversation with one of the keepers about lenses and the kind of light they had. He also used a cane to get around. Gramps had been really tired all the time, but on the trip he had more energy, and I thought he might be improving." Instead, maybe he was using up all he had left. At least that was what it seemed like now.

"All right. Let's see if there are people here who might have met him." Hilliard pulled into the parking lot and turned off the engine, the roll of the ocean instantly replacing the hum.

Hilliard got out, and Brian did the same, realizing just how futile this whole thing might be. How in the heck were they going to find someone who remembered them after all this time and with the number of visitors a place like this got? Brian wasn't sure what he was going to say, but he followed Hilliard up to the house and visitor center.

"Excuse me," Hilliard asked a man outside with a name badge. The light was still in use as a navigational aid, so it had official keepers, which Brian thought was pretty awesome. "I'm hoping you can help us. I know this is a long shot, but my friend and his grandfather visited here on a trip down the coast about three years ago or so. Would there be anyone here who might remember them?"

At least the man, who was about their age, didn't dismiss them right away or laugh. "I've been here two years because the last keeper retired. He moved out east, as far as I know." He pulled off his hat and scratched his head. "Sorry." He shifted his gaze to look up at the top of the light, and Brian did the same, hoping for some sort of inspiration.

"Can I ask, do you have security cameras?" Hilliard asked.

"Sure do. Had to install them a few years ago. Even out here, we have issues sometimes."

Hilliard smiled. "How far back do the files go?"

The man nodded. "I see. Sorry. We only keep a few months, and then the files are discarded to make room for newer ones. But I can check. Sometimes the old keeper kept stuff he didn't need to. I've been cleaning some stuff out but haven't gotten to that yet."

Brian wasn't hopeful, but the date was etched in his mind. He gave it to the keeper, who went inside to check.

"I don't know how much this whole thing is going to help. The coast out here is really rugged. That's what Gramps liked. We were away from tons of people, and we just drove. There aren't many more places like this." Which is why it had been so easy to pin the crime on him in the first place.

"We'll figure something out. If you don't look, then you don't find anything." Hilliard seemed so sure of himself. Brian wished he could have that kind of confidence.

The keeper returned, shaking his head. "I'm sorry. I don't have anything from around that date."

"Well, thank you for looking," Hilliard said. Brian thanked him as well before heading back toward the car. Maybe he just wasn't meant to be cleared. Maybe it was his destiny to carry this around with him for the rest of his life.

"Hey," Hilliard said as he strode to the car. "It's okay. This sort of thing happens." He pulled open the door and slid behind the wheel.

Brian got in, wanting to ask Hilliard to just take him home. This entire exercise was futile; he should have seen that from the start.

"There's nothing out here for us," Brian said softly, staring out toward the ocean.

"You don't know that." Hilliard squeezed his knee, and when Brian turned toward him, he was met with a hopeful smile. Then Hilliard kissed him lightly. "We have to try. If someone remembers you, then we have a major hole in the case, and it's a significant enough development to petition the courts. If we can establish a solid alibi, then we'll get the court to take notice and provide the evidence to the police to get them on our side and convince them to reopen the burglary case." He seemed so excited that Brian found himself feeling the same way. Hilliard's energy and outlook were contagious.

"Okay," he said, flashing a small smile.

"Good." Hilliard slid his hand around the back of Brian's neck and gently tugged him forward. He leaned closer, kissing him hard, sending Brian's mind into a spin. He had no idea how Hilliard could affect him this way, but every time Hilliard kissed him, Brian felt like he could fly. When Hilliard paused, he breathed deeply, eyes wide. "I think I'm going to have to do that every time we don't find anything."

"Huh?" Brian said, blinking, trying to make sense of what he said.

"It's simple. Whenever we get unhelpful news, I kiss you. Make the most of a bad situation." He started the engine and backed out of the parking spot to head down the drive and out along the point toward the main road. Brian sat in the passenger seat, just watching Hilliard. There was something about him that made everything seem okay. Brian didn't know if he could trust or believe it, but it was there. Damn, he wished he could believe what Hilliard did—that everything would be fine. But his experience was something completely different.

At the end of the point, Hilliard turned south. "Where did you and Gramps stop next?"

"We stopped for lunch a ways south and drove as far as Point Reyes to the next lighthouse. I'll show you when we get there."

Hilliard sped up, the air blew through his hair, and Brian sat back to try to enjoy the ride.

"ARE YOU sure this is the place?" Hilliard asked as he pulled into a diner that looked to be from a different era.

"Yeah. Gramps liked the place. He said it reminded him of a diner he used to eat at when he was a kid. The food was pretty good." Brian got out of the car, and they went inside.

"Is anyone familiar? I know it's been a while." Hilliard sat in a booth, and Brian took the place across from him.

"There was a server that Gramps talked with for quite a while. She was older, and it was quiet, so she settled in for a good talk while we waited for our food." He wished he could remember her name. She and Gramps had enjoyed talking about the way things used to be, and it was possible that she might remember them. "I don't see her. All the people working here look young." And like they hadn't had a good meal in a long time.

"What I get you?" a woman asked in a heavy accent.

"There used to be an older lady who worked here a while ago. Really friendly?" Brian asked.

The server shrugged.

"Lisa?" the other server offered quietly. "She doesn't work here anymore. The place was sold a while ago." She had less of an Asian accent, but her eyes were as sunken as the other woman's, and her skin as sallow. Neither of them looked healthy. Brian's appetite went south, and Hilliard leaned forward.

"Thank you," he said softly. Both women glanced toward a door at the back of the dining area, fear in their eyes. Brian was about to get up when Hilliard lifted his phone so the women could see it. Brian didn't know what he was showing them, but the women looked at each other and then turned away. Hilliard slipped his phone in his pocket, and the second woman brought them each a glass of Sprite.

Brian wondered what that was about, but Hilliard's expression told him he shouldn't ask and just drink. Hilliard pulled out some money and paid for the drinks, finishing his Sprite before leaving a tip and thanking the women. Then he motioned to the door, and Brian finished his drink as well. He and Hilliard got in the car, and they headed away.

"Okay. What was that about? I hate Sprite. And what was with your phone?"

He unlocked it and passed it over. The screen read: *Need Help? Sprite = Yes, Water = No.* He handed it back to Hilliard.

"Those women were scared to death, and I doubt they're being fed properly. And something had to be going on, so I thought I would ask without raising suspicion. If the boss thought I was onto what was happening, he'd cause a lot of trouble."

"God," Brian breathed, realizing that Hilliard was probably understating things. It was likely that the women would simply disappear. "What do we do?"

"The last time I flew into California, every time I went to the airport bathroom or public restroom, there was a sign in English and Spanish with a number to call if you need help. When we come into reception again, see if you can find a picture of it and we'll call that number. Jot down the name and location of the restaurant so we don't forget it, and we'll see if we can help."

"You did this without raising suspicion, didn't you?" He was slick and maybe a little sneaky.

"The boss was just in the back, and he might have ways of either watching them or listening to them, so I tried to make this as unobtrusive as possible."

"But how do you know they're telling the truth?" Brian asked.

"Desperation and fear. Both of them reeked of it. Who knows what happened? Maybe they were trafficked into the country and are now working off some debt for pennies an hour. I represented a whole family back in Cleveland who had been taken advantage of. I was able to help them, but Alan was angry because they couldn't pay." Hilliard shook his head. "He turned out to be a real asshole. I always wanted to be a partner in a large law firm, one big enough that I could take the occasional case just because it was the right thing to do. When we started the firm, I had visions of growing it into something special, a firm we could be proud of and one that would eventually become what I had always envisioned, one that could help people like those women in the diner. But Alan, my ex-partner and jerk extraordinaire ex-boyfriend, squashed that vision like a bug."

"Sounds like he really was a dick," Brian said as he watched his phone. When they came into the next small town, he got a signal and found the number. Brian called, and Hilliard pulled over. Brian let him explain what he'd suspected and what he'd done.

"That's good. … Yes." He explained things once more, describing the women, then smiled. "I'm glad you can help." He ended the call and pulled back onto the road. "It's a state agency, and they said they would have someone out there and that they knew just how to handle the situation."

"But—"

"They assured me that their people understood what they needed to do and that they would be careful to make sure the women stayed safe and were going to be treated well and get the help they needed."

He continued driving. For the moment, at least, Brian was much more worried about the women than he was about himself. "Where did you stop next?"

"At the lighthouse in Point Reyes. Gramps wanted to see it, but when we got there, he wasn't able to actually get to the light. There are a lot of stairs from the visitor center down to the light itself. He was able to see it from the center, though."

"That seems like a shame. This was a trip for your grandfather."

"I know. But it's, like, three hundred steps, and there was no way he could've made it. But Gramps found ways to keep himself occupied. He insisted that I make the trip and take pictures for him. So I went down, took pictures on my phone, and sent them to his phone."

Hilliard pulled off to the side of the road. "Do you still have those? And the texts?"

Brian nodded. "Yeah. I'm sure I do. I don't delete things like that. I tried to show that to my lawyer and the police, but they weren't interested and discounted it as proof of nothing."

Hilliard shook his head. "We'll get images of those when we get back. They were wrong, and your lawyer was inept. That's all I can say about that. He should have been looking for anything to help you. That was his job. It could help build our case that you were elsewhere. It probably isn't enough to conclusively show that you were here because it would only mean that someone with your phone took the pictures, but they could help bolster the case." He pulled back on the road. They turned inland for a ways until they came to the turnoff for Point Reyes and then entered the national park. Brian wondered in passing if they kept track of cars that came and went, but figured that was too much to hope for. They made the twenty-mile drive out toward the light.

"I can't believe you're doing all this to help me," Brian said as they reached the visitor center. They had already been on the road for a couple of hours and would still have the entire drive back.

"Stop. If there's a way to prove you were with your grandfather, then we will." He patted Brian's leg. "Now, since we're here, why don't we go on out to the light and see if there is anyone who might remember you."

Brian got out and joined a group of others as they made their way down the path. He hadn't been kidding about the stairs. It took them ten minutes or so to get down the path and the cliff face to the actual outcropping where the light stood. A ranger was giving a general talk about the light and when it was built. No one seemed familiar, but that wasn't a surprise. It had been years, and hundreds of people visited every day.

Brian went out to see the light itself more closely and realized that Hilliard wasn't with him. He paused to look for him but went on, getting a good look at the lens before wandering around the equipment building. By the time he reached the trailhead once more, he found Hilliard speaking to one of the rangers.

"I wouldn't ask if it wasn't important," Hilliard said as he approached. The ranger went inside and returned a few minutes later shaking his head. "Well, thank you. I knew it was a long shot." Hilliard turned away.

"What?"

"They have cameras because of security and the foot traffic, but they only keep the footage for six months and rotate it out." He shrugged.

"It's going to be that way everywhere," Brian told him. "It isn't like anyone is going to remember me or Gramps after all this time, and even if they think they do, they aren't going to be able to testify to it. Too much time has passed." He turned toward the steps and the trek back to the car. "We might as well head back. There isn't any more to see."

"Okay. But we aren't giving up. There has to be a way. We just need to find it." Hilliard started back up the steps, and Brian sighed. They had found nothing, and yet it had been a very long time since anyone had been so stubborn for his benefit and in his defense. One thing was for sure: if there was a way to prove he was innocent, Hilliard was determined to figure out what it was.

Chapter 7

"DO YOU want a beer or something?" Hilliard asked Brian once they were back in town. It was well after dinnertime, and Hilliard was more than a little hungry. He led the way inside, and Brian flopped down on his great-aunt's fussy sofa. The old piece of furniture groaned but stayed in one piece.

"I could use one… or three about now." Brian held his head. "Sorry for being a downer."

Hilliard got two bottles from the refrigerator and handed one to Brian. "For a guy who didn't think we had much chance…."

Brian nodded. "I guess I was putting more hope into finding something than I thought. I guess I had really wondered if there might be something to help me. And the answer is there might have been at the time, if anyone had looked. I had no idea what I should do, and my appointed attorney—"

"Didn't do his job," Hilliard interjected. "And now the information that could have proven your innocence is gone. At least to the south. You said that you went north too."

"We did. We went south first and then continued past Mendocino on the way back and headed north for a while. But we can't do that today."

"My question is, how did you do all that in a single day?"

"Gramps was always an early riser, so we left first thing in the morning, and Gramps slept part of the way on the return trip north, so by the time we got back here in the afternoon, he had energy and wanted to keep going."

Hilliard leaned forward. "When was the burglary supposed to have happened?" He was trying to build a more accurate picture of the day's events.

"They said between approximately twelve thirty and three in the afternoon."

"So the burglary likely happened while you and Gramps were north of town." He mentally chastised himself for not seeing that sooner. He should have been more in tune with the details. Proving his presence at Point Arena or Point Reyes might not have provided Brian with a rock-solid alibi. Still, it would have proven that Brian's story was true and helped bolster his case.

"So…?"

"The trip south is less important than what you did afterwards." He couldn't help smiling. "Don't worry. We aren't beaten yet. But I think we need to be smarter this time." He jumped up and grabbed a pad of paper, then sat next to Brian. "Write down everything you can remember about that day, including where you stopped and anyone you might have seen."

"But is this really going to do anything?" Brian asked.

"Going north is closer to home. You live here, but I'm sure you spend time in Fort Bragg—everyone seems to. It's got the only full-service grocery store. Maybe you saw one of Gramps's friends, or someone you knew from high school. All we need is one person to remember you with your grandfather and we're home free." He sat back with a smile. "Just try to think about it."

Brian began writing, and Hilliard watched as the dejected set of his shoulders lifted. "And what if we do find someone?" He paused, intense eyes once again filling with hope. Hilliard wished he could make him look that way all the time. Seeing Brian downtrodden tugged at his heart and made him angry at the same time. If the appropriate people had done their jobs, Brian would not be in this position.

"Then we get them to make a statement and go from there." Hilliard knew he needed to put in his request to the California bar to complete their process for membership. He had already researched it and had the materials he needed to prepare.

"But what if we don't find anything?" Brian asked.

"Then we keep looking. There's something out there that will lead us to proving your innocence and to the real thief. We just have to find it." He lightly bumped Brian's shoulder. "Don't worry, I'm not going to give up." Those words sent a chill running through him.

"You look pale," Brian said softly. Hilliard tried to wipe his expression clean but obviously failed. "What is it?"

"Nothing you can help with, I promise." Everyone had regrets, and one of Hilliard's biggest was one of his first clients. He had given up, thinking there was nothing else to find. But there had been, and if he had looked further, he could have spared his client and their family a great deal of heartache. The facts came to light eventually, but Hilliard always regretted that he hadn't dug deeper and uncovered them sooner. "Just an old regret that I can't do a damned thing about."

"We all have those. I don't regret taking Gramps on that road trip. He enjoyed himself, and that was what was really important, no matter how things turned out. If I had a choice, I'd probably do the same thing again. Regardless of what happened to me, Gramps had a good time, and we had a final great day together."

Hilliard put an arm around his shoulders, and Brian leaned closer. Turning toward him, Brian smiled slightly, and Hilliard kissed him, unable to restrain himself. As much as he kept telling himself that he needed to take things slowly and that he was just getting over the crap show that was his relationship with Alan, being with Brian felt right.

He pressed Brian back against the cushions, shifting his weight so their kiss deepened. It was so easy to get lost in a moment like this with Brian, especially when he slipped his hand under Hilliard's shirt, warmth spreading around him from where his hand slid over his belly.

Brian broke their kiss, both of them breathing deeply, Hilliard's eyes a little unfocused. "You know, this may be the wrong thing to be doing."

Hilliard held still. "We can stop if that's what you want."

"No." Brian groaned and pulled him back down, their lips crashing together in a frenzy of need. Hilliard tugged at Brian's shirt, pulling it upward. As soon as it was high enough, he stroked his belly, then sucked at a pert nipple while Brian arched his back, pressing his chest forward, groaning deeply. Brian tasted of fresh air and sunshine mixed with a heady hint of sweat and man. It was perfection, and Hilliard licked his way to the other pec, growling as he swirled his tongue around the stiffened bud. He slipped his hands around Brian, holding him tightly as heat and desire built.

A vibration between them made him pause. "Is that your heart?" Hilliard asked. Brian groaned and shook his head. "I didn't think so." He sat back, and Brian pulled his phone from his pocket.

"It's Gran." Brian answered the call. "Okay. Stay calm. I'm on my way." Brian hung up and got to his feet. "Gran isn't feeling well. I need to take her into the hospital in Fort Bragg." He headed for the door, the beers they had barely touched sitting on the table.

"Come on." Hilliard led Brian out the front door and to the car, pulling away just after Brian had closed his door. It wasn't far, but he got Brian there fast and followed him inside.

"What's wrong?" Brian asked.

"I'm really cold," she said from her chair, under a blanket. The dogs huddled nearby. "And my head is a little spinny."

"Okay." Brian took Gran's hand. "What did you have for lunch?"

"I wasn't very hungry," she answered.

Brian nodded. "Hilliard, there's some apple juice in the refrigerator and some crackers on the counter. Can you bring them?"

He hurried to the kitchen, poured a glass of juice, and grabbed the crackers. Brian took the glass as soon as he returned and helped her drink. He also handed her a cracker, which she ate and washed down with more juice.

"Do you feel like you're going to be sick?" Brian asked, and Beverly shook her head once, then stilled with a soft sigh.

"Then eat a little more," he told her. Beverly finished the cracker and the glass of juice. Hilliard got some more and returned as Beverley finished the second cracker and started eating a third. He handed Brian the glass, and she drank some more. "Are you starting to warm up?"

"Yes." She breathed deeply before settling more quietly in the chair.

"I'm going to heat up something for us to eat." He and Hilliard left her with the crackers and headed to the kitchen. "She skipped lunch, and her blood sugar went too low. It's happened a few times before." He pulled out a container of pasta from the refrigerator and put it in the microwave. "I left this for her to reheat."

"Maybe she just forgot," Hilliard said.

Brian nodded as he took the pasta out of the microwave, stirred it, and put the container on a plate. He took it all to the living room and handed it to Beverly, who began eating right away.

"I hope you're feeling better," Hilliard told her.

"I am." She took a bite and sat back while she chewed. "I hate getting old. You know?" She ate some more, and some of her sparkle returned. Her cheeks had more color, and she settled the blanket over her lap. "In my mind, I'm still thirty and can do all the things I did then. But I can't anymore. I get up and look in the mirror, wondering where the old lady came from. And now that I'm over eighty, I wonder where the time went." She took Brian's hand. "You two are young, and you need to make the most of it. Go out and do all those fun things I can't anymore."

"Gran, you just need to rest."

"Yeah, and tomorrow I'll bring the car over and all three of us can go for a Sunday drive with the top down," Hilliard offered. "It's supposed to be nice."

"You young people don't need to include an old lady in your fun," she said.

"You're only as old as you want to be," he told her and got a smile in response. "It will be fun."

She patted Hilliard's arm and went back to her dinner. Hilliard figured he'd get himself something to eat on the way out and leave them to their dinner. He said good night to Brian, knowing he was going to need to stay with Beverly. "I'll come by late tomorrow morning."

"Sounds good," Brian said, opening the front door. "Hurry before the dogs decide to make a run for it." He closed the door behind them and stood on the front stoop. "I'm sorry about all this."

"You need to take care of her. It's perfectly okay." Hilliard lightly cupped Brian's cheeks and kissed him, not holding anything back. "Just a taste for next time." He smiled and headed down the walk, keenly aware of Brian watching as he made his way home.

"ARE YOU ready to go?" Hilliard asked late the following morning. He'd had a largely sleepless night where his mind refused to turn off, alternating between dreams of stripping the handyman naked and how he was going to prove him innocent. It was a weird combination that only added to his restlessness. He'd only managed to get some rest once the sun began making an appearance.

Beverly approached on Brian's arm, and he opened the door and brought the seatback forward before moving the passenger seat as far forward as it would go. "I'll sit in back," Beverly said as Brian began to climb in. "I'll be perfectly comfortable and can spread out if I need to."

"No. I'll get in back and you sit in the front." Brian got in back, and she slowly got in and settled. Brian handed her a blanket, which she put over her legs, and then Hilliard went around to the driver's side. "Where are we going?"

"Well, I thought we'd head toward Fort Bragg. We can go out to the lighthouse there. I understand you can drive most of the way out, so we should get a really nice view. Then we can continue north a little and take in the rugged coast. Maybe get a late lunch at Noyo River Grill."

"Their shrimp is amazing," Gran said. "Or it used to be. It's been a while since I've been there."

"They moved to the top of the bluff, but last time I ate there, it was the same," Brian said as Hilliard pulled out.

"If the wind gets to be too much, we can put the top up," Hilliard offered as they headed through town and out toward the highway.

"Don't you dare. It's a beautiful day, and I haven't been in one of these since Chester and I had one in the seventies. There is just something very California about a convertible." They shared a smile as Hilliard made the turn north with the sun just peeking through the clouds.

Hilliard loved riding with the top down, and Brian seemed in better spirits today. Beverly seemed happy too as they crossed the river and rounded the curve that led down to the Pacific. "I love this drive," Brian said. "I make it more often than I probably need to, but it has a great view."

"You bet it does," Beverly said. They continued through the roundabout before crossing the river gorge that signaled the beginning of Fort Bragg. Hilliard continued past the Skunk Train depot and out north, continuing into the coastal redwoods.

"How far do you want to go? This part of the coast is pretty rugged, and there isn't a lot up here."

"It's okay. We have a full tank of gas and nowhere we need to be for a while." After about forty-five minutes, Hilliard pulled to a stop at an overlook to let everyone take in the view of the ruggedly rocky coast with cliffs that went over a hundred feet down to the sea.

"Now, that's a view," Beverly said softly. "I used to like to take a swim every now and then in the Pacific."

"Isn't it too cold?" Hilliard asked.

"We didn't have much choice. It wasn't like there were other good places. So we'd swim… and yes, I almost froze my butt off." She led the laughter, with Brian and him joining in. "When I got older, I got a wetsuit and we'd go surfing. Your grandfather was quite a sight on a board."

"Gramps surfed?" Brian asked. "I didn't know that."

"Sure. Why do you think I fell for him? He was so handsome and every bit a surfer when he was young, with long hair and a body that would stop traffic." She hooted. "He and I used to take our vacation time and follow the waves. Went to Hawaii a few times, riding waves on the North Shore. Big waves sometimes. But as happens with everyone, we got older, developed responsibilities… and we settled in Mendo where he could be close to the ocean."

"Gramps was always good with his hands. He made a number of the furniture pieces in Gran's house, and he worked on a number of the places in town to help restore them over the years. It's possible he worked in your house at some point or other."

Hilliard liked that his house had a connection to Brian's family.

Beverly nodded. "Probably. In his later years, he was always helping friends out. Chester was a good man, and I miss him."

Brian took her hand. "I do too."

Hilliard was quiet for a little while, letting the two of them have their moment. "I hate to ask, but I need some information. Brian and Chester were out together all day. Could someone have planned the burglary and decided to pin it on you because they knew you were gone? Who had advance notice of the trip?" His mind churned over the little they knew.

Brian and Beverly looked at each other. "No one, I don't think. Gramps had been feeling tired, and we had talked about going, but he got up that morning saying he felt good and asked to go, so we got in the car and off we went. It was a spur-of-the-moment kind of thing."

That told Hilliard a little more, and he turned to Beverly. "Did you tell anyone about the trip?"

"It was a Sunday, so people asked me why Chester wasn't in church, and I said he was out with Brian. Then, later that afternoon while Violet was at her ladies' circle meeting, someone broke into the house and stole what they could carry." She seemed down.

Hilliard took her hand. "You did nothing wrong. But it sounds to me as though we should definitely be looking closer to Violet for the real thief, because it seems like whoever broke in knew that she wasn't going to be home." His mind was already churning over possibilities, even though he had zero suspects and still no way to prove that Brian hadn't committed the burglary. "What also bothers me is how they planted the evidence with your fingerprints on it."

"They could have lifted the print from somewhere. That's always possible, and the evidence wasn't in my truck until afterwards. I know it wasn't there on that Sunday, but by Tuesday, suddenly the police are finding a stolen item in my truck and I'm being arrested for burglary. I can't prove where I was, Gran was dealing with Gramps's funeral, and…." He lowered his head. "I don't ever want to feel that lost again," Brian added roughly, his voice scratching.

Beverly reached for his hand. "I never thought you were guilty for a second."

"I know." He placed his hand in hers, and Hilliard gave the two of them a minute.

"So what are we going to do next?" Beverly asked. "This shit can't stand." God, he loved her steel backbone.

"You were going to find me a way to talk to Violet, and we need to get a copy of the original police report. We need to know what they found at the scene of the burglary and what they might have overlooked. Then we can talk to any suspects we have and see if we can rattle one of them."

"How?" Beverly and Brian asked together.

"What is their worst nightmare?" Hilliard asked. "We let them know that Brian has been proven innocent—that there is new evidence and that he was elsewhere at the time of the burglary. That is the guilty party's worst nightmare. And we can use the Mendocino grapevine to do that little bit of work for us. Especially if Beverly is willing to start the ball rolling." He might not know much about the town yet, but Beverly certainly did, and he had an idea that she would know exactly who to talk to in order to get tongues wagging.

"But we haven't proven where I was," Brian said.

"That's the beauty. They don't know that. We've made a bit of a show of going up and down the coast. We rode through town with the top down past some of the ladies."

"Yeah. I loved that. Violet is such a bitch sometimes."

"Gran," Brian groaned almost comically.

"Well, she is. Those grandchildren of hers are such entitled brats, and her children are no better." Beverly snapped her pocketbook open. "I made a list of all her relatives in town. We can start with these. I wouldn't put it past any of them to go in and take what they wanted. They're a greedy lot, just like Violet. The apple doesn't fall far from the tree, if you ask me." She passed it over, and Hilliard took a look at the list, with its small, wavering script. "Now, where else did you and Chester go on your trip?"

"We stopped at the Point Cabrillo Light. I drove him out, and we spent some time in the shop looking at the lens and other fittings. That was most fascinating to Gramps, being able to see it up close."

"Then let's go," Beverly said. "I know it's a slim chance, but we need to find out if they can tell us anything or remember either of you. God, I feel younger than I have in years."

Brian reached forward. "Try not to overdo it, okay?" He seemed pale, and his eyes filled with worry. Hilliard could only imagine how he must be feeling at that moment.

"I'm not going anywhere, so you can let that worry go. I'm not going to die like Chester. He had a bad heart, and the last I checked, the doctor said mine was just fine." She patted his hand. "Now, let's go."

"Aye, aye, captain," Hilliard said as they headed south back toward Fort Bragg. He drove as quickly as he dared, and they made the turn out to the lighthouse. He slowed to a crawl as pedestrians filled the roadway. Beverly waved and smiled like she was the queen in a parade.

"What if there's no help here either? What do we do?" Brian asked.

"Then we look deeper. Proof is out there somewhere, and we'll find it," Hilliard told him as they passed a large group of kids. He went by them slowly before pulling into a small parking area near the lighthouse.

The light was very traditional, the tower in front, with the small keeper's residence attached, painted light yellow with tan trim. It wasn't very tall, but it stood on the high bluff, and Hilliard imagined it could be seen for miles out at sea.

Beverly said, "You go on inside. I'm going to stay here and enjoy the quiet."

"Are you sure you don't want to come in?" Hilliard asked.

"No," she answered gently. "Chester loved this place. He even worked on repairs after a storm. It was special to him, and…." She lowered her gaze. Hilliard didn't want to push her. "I'll stay here."

He nodded and joined Brian outside the building. "Is this too hard?" Hilliard asked quietly.

"In some ways. It's been like saying goodbye to Gramps all over again." Hilliard got the feeling Brian hadn't had much of a chance to grieve the loss of his grandfather. "But what am I going to do, fall to pieces right here?"

Hilliard tossed him the keys. "If you want, put the top up and sit with your grandmother." He had an idea that this was affecting both of them more deeply than either wanted to admit.

"I'll be okay. I need to do this." Brian pressed the keys back into Hilliard's hand. "Let's go." He led the way inside and began looking around while Hilliard paused near the door before approaching the lady at the register, who was about his age and with a name tag that read Bridget. "Excuse me, but that sign…." He pointed to the one regarding security camera in use. "Is that real?"

She smiled and indicated a camera in the corner before leaning slightly forward. "We had some people a few years ago who caused a lot of problems, so the board had a camera installed to deter them." She sighed. "Not that they use the recordings for anything."

"But I suppose they could if something happened," Hilliard prompted.

"They could if they knew what they were doing. The problem is that no one used the information, and it just keeps building up on the system. I've been trying to help them put a retention system in place, but the most they did was have the cameras shut off when we're closed."

Hilliard smiled. "So you have multiple years of video?"

"They did some cleanup in the beginning, but yeah. It's compressed on the server, but we have gobs of it. Why?"

Hilliard could barely breathe. "Would it be possible to see it? I have the date and approximate time." He grinned because this was almost too good to be true and he didn't want to get his hopes up.

"Why?" Bridget asked.

"I'm a lawyer, but not here in California yet. The thing is, a friend of mine was accused of a crime he didn't commit. And the day of the crime, he was here with his grandfather, who passed away right afterwards. Your video could be the way we can prove he was here."

"You're serious?" she asked, and Hilliard nodded.

"Can you help me?"

"Let me get someone to take the register," she said and called to the other lady in the shop, who took over. Then she got a laptop from under the counter and logged in.

"We should get out of her way." Bridget led Hilliard to one of the shaded benches just outside. Hilliard signaled to Brian, who joined them.

Hilliard gave her the date and approximate time. She brought up the file for that day and began scrolling through. She slowed the video.

"That's me, and there's Gramps. We must have just arrived."

They continued forwarding the video as the lady at the register helped various visitors. About a half an hour after they first appeared, Brian and his grandfather appeared again, with his grandfather buying something and shoving the receipt into his pocket before taking the sweatshirt with him.

"He was a little cold, since the clouds were rolling in," Brian said, glued to the images on the screen, while Hilliard checked the time. In the video, it was a little before two in the afternoon. Both Brian and his grandfather then left and made no additional appearances on camera.

"Is that what you needed?" Bridget asked. "Did it help?"

"Yes, a lot. Can we get a copy of this file?" Hilliard said with a grin. "Brian, go back in the gift shop and buy one of those turtle-shaped USB drives." He opened his wallet and pulled out a couple of twenties. "And put these in the donation box." He would do just about anything to make Bridget happy.

"When he gets back, I'll give you a copy of the file," she agreed. "And I'll make an extra copy here so it will be available." She typed some, and when Brian returned, she inserted the drive and added the file. "You have to promise to come back and let me know how things work out."

"We will," Brian said when she handed him the drive. "This could clear my name." He was practically shaking.

"Thank you, Bridget. We really appreciate it." Hilliard shook her hand as she got up from the bench and closed the laptop. Brian hurried back to the car, with Hilliard following.

"We got it," Brian said. "They had old video."

"Apparently they never cleared their camera system after they installed it." Hilliard took the drive, made sure the cover was on it, and slipped it into his pocket.

"So you were here and you can prove it," Beverly said.

"To a large degree, but don't get your hopes up." Dammit, Hilliard hated throwing cold water on their happiness, but technically it was still possible for Brian to have done it, at least as far as the timeline was concerned. "We have a long way to go."

Chapter 8

"WHAT DO you mean?" Brian felt like the rug had been pulled out from under him—again. "Gramps and I were there. The video is time-stamped. What more do they want?"

"Calm down," Gran said. "Let Hilliard get us out of here, and then we can talk it all through." She leaned back, and Hilliard started the car and drove slowly back to the main road. Hilliard made the turn back to Fort Bragg and pulled into the parking lot of the restaurant. Brian wasn't hungry, but Gran probably was.

Brian was still steaming and wanted some answers. "So what gives?" he pressed as soon as they stopped.

"Okay. The burglary took place between twelve thirty and about three, when Violet got home from the ladies' group meeting. You and Gramps appeared on tape about one seventeen and then appeared once more a little before two. The prosecutor will argue that you could have gotten back to Mendo and broken into the place before she got home, especially since you would have known the schedule because of your grandmother. It's stretching it, so we could argue how preposterous that is. What we found is great. It isn't a slam dunk, but it's close."

"Okay," Brian said, his insides still churning, but at least he felt better. "So what's next? We try to find out who really did it?"

"No. We try to see if we can find the receipt for the purchase your grandfather made. Do you think that's possible? It looked like he kept the receipt."

"And after we went to Point Cabrillo, we got something to eat at Noyo River Grill. Gramps insisted on paying since I did all the driving, but you know him, he always paid cash."

"And he probably shoved the receipt in his pocket."

"Chester always did that. I was forever cleaning his daily crap out of his pockets."

Hilliard continued, "Do you still have the clothes he was wearing? Don't worry if you haven't. I'd expect that you would have gone through his things."

Gran looked so fragile as she shook her head. "I have some of his things in a box upstairs under the bed. I couldn't throw out everything. It was like letting him go all over again. But I only kept mementos of our time together, not receipts."

"It's okay, Gran. We can look through that when we get back." Sometimes his life felt like he was taking two steps forward and one step back. "And if it isn't there?"

"Then we'll look at other ways of narrowing down the timeline." Hilliard opened the door and got out. "Let's go have some lunch and celebrate a little. We found something big, and the rest is narrowing things down."

"DO YOU think it's possible that the receipt is still in the house?" Brian asked once they got back home and Gran lay down for a nap.

"I don't know. It depends on what Beverly kept. But either way, the video we found proves your story was true from the beginning, and it puts you at Point Cabrillo well inside the time that the burglary took place. If a jury had seen this evidence the first time around, you would not have been convicted, and the police would have been forced to look at other suspects."

Hilliard had stopped by his house to grab his laptop before bringing them to Gran's, so he plugged in the drive and downloaded the video to his computer. He brought it up and scrolled through it once more, finding where Brian and Gramps entered and then where they came in once more. "I'm just making detailed timeline notes. I want to build as much detail as I possibly can to see where the holes are." He continued watching and smiled.

"Look, isn't that your grandfather yet again? Right there." Hilliard brought the video in closer. It got a little blurry, but Gramps and his cane could be made out. "What was he doing?"

"I don't know." They replayed it.

"He's unwrapping a candy of some sort. Yeah, he's eating something."

"I bet he came back inside because I was out wandering the cliffs looking for sea lions and he needed to be out of the sun." It was that simple, and that also meant they didn't leave the lighthouse until after two o'clock.

"That makes it even tighter." Hilliard made more notes and then continued the video, but there was nothing more to see.

Brian sat next to him as Hilliard continued working. "Okay. Beverly said the ladies' group meets at twelve thirty and that they are done by three. If that's the case, then getting to the lighthouse before one thirty would mean that you would have to have done the deed, picked up your grandfather, gotten him in the car, driven down to the lighthouse, and gotten down that road with all the people out for a Sunday stroll, parked, and had your grandfather out of the car and into the gift shop in less than an hour. I would doubt that. And even that would mean pushing it hard, especially with your grandfather using a cane."

"Gramps didn't move fast—Gran can vouch for that. You can see in the video that each step was measured."

"True. So that leaves you getting him in the car, driving back, and dropping him off. You could do that in half an hour if you put him right in the car and took him home, because there's less walking and you just had to get him in the car. No fussing and stuff. So that would leave a half hour or so for you to do the deed. Even that's stretching it, considering what we're talking about, but it's possible, I suppose. I've seen lawyers make more preposterous leaps stick. But this does verify your story, and it incriminates the police who botched the investigation." Hilliard sat back. "You said that you had a late lunch after you left in Fort Bragg, so let's look at that to button this up."

"But what do we do otherwise?" Brian asked.

"We get Gran to talk to some of the ladies at church. She can tell them that we've found evidence that proves you didn't do the burglary and that we can motion to have the conviction vacated. With new findings, it's unlikely the DA would retry the case, and I can petition to have the conviction expunged. That will spread through her circles like wildfire, especially if Beverly has an I-told-you-so attitude. After a couple of days, the truth will be everywhere, including making it to the actual thieves."

"Okay."

"Also, be sure to lock your truck, and if you have any sort of alarm, set it. I wouldn't put it past the thief to try to throw suspicion back on you. The truck trick worked before, so they could try again. Take pictures of the truck at night, all that sort of thing. In the morning, if you find anything, call me and then the police." He closed his laptop. "Once the rumor has a chance to spread, you and I will pay Violet a visit." He crossed his arms over his chest, smiling smugly.

"She won't let me in the house."

Hilliard lightly stoked his cheek. "She will when she sees the video." He leaned closer. "I always knew you could never hurt anyone, and now we have proof, and we're going to make sure everyone knows it."

Brian closed his eyes, holding Hilliard's hand. "But what if the thief comes after me or Gran?" He could take care of himself, but Gran was another matter. "It's always possible. They thought they got away with it, and now there will be people looking around again. It could stir up a hornet's nest."

Hilliard met his gaze. "I don't have an answer for you. I honestly don't think that will happen. But what we do is up to you and to Beverly. It has to be you who make the decisions."

"Don't you dare," Gran said from the living room doorway, and Brian stiffened and jumped back. "You are not stopping. We are so close to proving your innocence, and we have to have some backbone. No one is going to hurt me." She slowly sat down in her chair, sighing when she finally settled.

"But Gran—" he began, and she cut him off.

"That's enough. We're going to go through with this. Now, you make sure your truck is secured and do all the things Hilliard suggested. I'll keep my doors locked and watch out for prowlers." She closed her eyes. "We need to figure out who might have done this, and no backing down now." She had always had a fierce streak, and Brian knew better than to argue with her.

"I thought you were napping." Brian figured he could change the subject. No matter what Gran said, he was still worried about any repercussions, especially toward Gran. She was the only family he had. She was getting older, and his time with her was limited. He didn't want to lose a second of it.

"And you two were canoodling on my sofa. What does that have to do with the price of tea in China?" She shook her head, and Hilliard chuckled next to him.

"She has you there."

"He agrees with me." She seemed way too self-satisfied.

"That we were canoodling on the sofa? Yeah, we were."

Gran leaned forward. "Neither of you is too big for me to take over my knee." She was nearly smiling, and her eyes sparkled. "That's enough of the teasing. What do you need me to do?"

"I DON'T know if I like putting Gran on the spot like that," Brian said that evening as they sat on Hilliard's back porch, each with a beer in hand, the marine layer fog in the air reflecting back the lights of the town.

"She's the only one who can do it because everyone will listen to her. Just relax. It's only a few phone calls and some talk after church. Besides, do you think now that we have proof of your alibi that she isn't going to crow about it a little? She never doubted the truth, and that says a lot."

Brian sipped his beer. "I know. I hung on to the fact that she believed me while I was in jail. It isn't that I worry about. She says she can get the police report." The question of how she was going to do that had his head spinning.

"Your grandmother has resources neither of us has. She's been here almost her entire life. She and your grandfather have a well of favors and goodwill to call in that neither of us does." He set the empty bottle beside his chair. "We've gone over this with her, and I don't think we need to do it again."

Brian wasn't convinced. "I'm worried, okay? I can deal with whatever comes my way, but I hate Gran being in the line of fire in any way."

"All she's going to do is tell a few friends that she was right and that we have proof of it. Then she says she has a way to get the police report and that we are not to ask anything more." Hilliard's lips quirked. "I keep wondering what your Gran has in mind. My brain keeps picturing something naughty, and every time it does, all I want to do is groan because I do not need to be thinking that about your grandmother."

Brian snickered. "Can you just imagine Gran calling the station to talk to a certain officer and offering to bake him some of her *cookies*?"

He did his best to make it sound dirty, and Hilliard cackled. "Or that she's hurrying over to the station to give him what he always wanted?"

Hilliard met his gaze. "I have to ask. You don't think she got us out of the house because she is going to lure over some officer near retirement that she's had her eye on for the past few months?"

Brian shivered. "I wouldn't put it past her. Not that there's anything wrong with her having a life after Gramps. Still…." He shivered again, and Hilliard pressed another bottle of beer into his hand. "Thanks. I think I needed that."

"No one wants to think about their parents having sex…."

"But your grandmother in a teddy heading down to the police station is more than I want to think about—ever."

Hilliard nearly did a spit take. "For the first part, wow, that's some imagination you have… and second, I did not need to have that image in my head." He opened the beer and drank. "I might need to get drunk to wipe it away."

Brian sipped his beer, and they settled into silence for a while. When he was in jail, silence and the dark were the enemy. It meant he had only his own thoughts to while away the hours, his mind repeating almost constantly that he didn't belong there, that he had done nothing wrong. But the silence with Hilliard felt completely different. Brian was comfortable and content, something he used to doubt he would ever feel again.

Hilliard placed his hand on top of Brian's, and he turned it over, entwining their fingers. "Have you decided what you're going to do with the house? Are you going to stay? You know you could sell it in a matter of days if you wanted." God, he hoped that Hilliard didn't intend to blow into town and then breeze out again like the rains that sometimes came through.

"I still haven't made any long-term plans. Every time I think about going back to Cleveland, my belly aches, and I know that isn't the right thing for me. So then I think about what I could do if I stayed here, and I wonder if I can make a living as a gay lawyer. My practice in Cleveland was pretty general. I have experience in a number of areas of the law, and I've applied for membership in the California bar, but it will take some time for them to review my application and paperwork, and I have to take an exam. The next one is scheduled in a few months, and I applied to sit for it."

"Are you nervous? Is that why you're hesitating?" Brian asked.

"No. I have the materials, and I'll spend a couple hours a day preparing. I should be fine. I passed the Ohio bar on the first try, but I'm not taking any chances." He paused. "I just don't seem to be able to make any decisions right now, though a plan is formulating in my mind." He brought Brian's hand to his lips and kissed it gently.

"Change sucks sometimes, and I understand how you feel. Your ex really hurt you, and it's only been a few months. But this house is yours, and it could be the basis of a good life here." It wasn't like he was asking Hilliard to commit to a life with him.

"I know. I think I just need some time and some stability. Taking the exam and being accepted to the bar here won't hurt my career or my standing in the profession. So I'm going to go forward while I think things through." He continued holding Brian's hand as he finished his beer.

"Is that partly why you haven't done anything?" Brian asked. "I mean, you kiss me like you want to devour me, and you set my head on fire, but you never do anything beyond that." He sat forward. "Is there something wrong with me?"

Hilliard set his bottle on the floor next to the others before turning toward him. "I don't know. I guess I thought that if we took things a little slow and didn't just jump into bed to hump our brains out, we could get to know each other first." He leaned closer, and Brian's heart beat hard enough that he wondered if Hilliard could hear it. "Besides, I mean, you're really sexy, and I found out that the last guy I was super attracted to cheated on me more times than I could count and that I was lucky not to have come down with anything because of it." He paused. "I think I'm a little gun-shy, and I don't want you to be a rebound sort of thing."

Brian sighed softly, his nervousness abating. "So that means…. I'm sorry, but sometimes I just need to know. I can't stand all the teenage kind of angst around relationships. I never could."

Hilliard smiled. "Me neither. So it means that I like you and I don't want to mess shit up."

"God, I'd like to smack Alan into the middle of next week. Sometimes relationships end, but you sit down and talk about it. You don't go running around behind someone's back." He clenched his fists, squeezing Hilliard's hand.

"I know you wouldn't do that, but…." Hilliard sighed.

"There's no hurry." It had been his own insecurities coming forward to smack him in the head. He relaxed once more, just watching the sky as the clouds moved closer to the ground.

They both jumped at a firm rap on the door, followed by additional pounding. For a second Brian was carried back to the day he was arrested and the police nearly beat down Gran's door. He breathed deeply as Hilliard got up and went through to the front door. "What's going on?" he asked, and then there was silence for a long time. "What are you doing here?"

At the tone, Brian went to see what was wrong.

Chapter 9

Hilliard glared at the man on his doorstep, trying to figure out why he looked so familiar.

"Aren't you going to invite me in? I should have known your mother would raise you like you were born in a barn." He stepped forward, but Hilliard began to close the door.

"Who the hell are you?" he asked when a hand pressed to the other side of the door Brian had just painted a few days ago.

"I'm your uncle," he snapped. "Now let me in. It's cold and damp out here."

"Timothy?" Hilliard asked. He hadn't seen him in years, and as far as he knew, his mother hadn't either. "I'll ask again what you're doing here. The way I was taught, guests *and* family call before they arrive."

Timothy humphed. "I'm not going to call when I visit my own house. Or what should be my house. I heard you were a lawyer." He leaned closer. "What underhanded trick did you use to get my mother to name you in her will? Whatever it is, you won't get away with it."

Hilliard had already had enough and felt Brian come up behind him. "I think it's time for you to leave. I didn't even know about the house until I was called by Grace's lawyer. So I think you can take yourself and your rotten entitled attitude and hit the road."

"You think you can get rid of me that easily?"

Hilliard chuckled. "You know, I think you just answered your own question. You're a prick, which is probably why Aunt Grace left the house to me. Now go away or the police will be called." He closed the door and locked it.

"What the hell was that?" Brian asked softly. "Was he really your uncle?"

"Of a sort. He was Great-Aunt Grace's only son. I remember him as being a demanding pain in the ass whenever we visited. Mom and I would come here, and he would hang around most of the time like he was jealous of us. Aunt Grace used to send him on his way, but the next day he'd be back."

A knock sounded again. Hilliard jumped, on edge. He peered out the window to Uncle Timothy lighting a cigarette. Never Tim, always Uncle Timothy. Hilliard went to the door, pulled it open, and glared at him. "What do you think is going to happen?" he snapped.

"The house is rightfully mine," he demanded, blowing smoke in Hilliard's direction.

"No, it's not. It was Aunt Grace's, and hers to do with as she liked. You can contact her lawyer, but I'm sure you'll find everything in order." He stepped closer, not about to be intimidated. "You can yell and bluster all you like, but it isn't going to change anything."

"We'll see about that," Timothy growled.

"Is that the best you have?" He shook his head. "A line from every pathetic villain in history? Please. Just go or I will call the police. I have a witness to your threats, so it will be an easy arrest. And because I have a witness, I will be making note of this little visit. You make another, and I'll take it to the police as a pattern of behavior." He knew exactly what he needed to do and had no intention of letting Timothy get away with anything.

"You think you know everything," he sputtered. "This should be my house. I grew up here, and Grace was my mother. She should have left the house to me."

Hilliard shrugged. "Yet she didn't. I wonder why." Just as he was coming to the end of his patience, Brian rested his hand gently on his back, and Hilliard felt calm and the tension eased away. "Just go."

"Where am I supposed to go? This is my home."

Hilliard shrugged, glancing back at Brian because he couldn't believe this guy was for real. "You have to be kidding me. You show up without calling, act like a jackass, and expect me to let you stay here? Are you crazy? You really have to be, because no sane person would act that way. There's a number of inns in town and up the road. Go there and see if they have a room." He shook his head, and this time he waited until Timothy got back in his car and drove away.

"That guy's cheese has fallen off his cracker," Brian said when Hilliard turned around. "He isn't really going to try to take the house?"

Hilliard shrugged. "He can try, but it isn't going to get very far. I don't know what he thinks he has to gain by acting that way. It isn't like

I'm going to say, 'Oh, hey, sorry, here, let me give you the house because you're such a nice guy.'" He rolled his eyes, and Brian snickered.

But then Brian paled. "Do you think this 'nice guy' is just going to go away? I knew guys like him when I was in jail. They think they're entitled to something, and it doesn't matter how irrational they are or if what you have has nothing to do with them. If they want something, they find a way to take it." His voice was so soft, Hilliard had to strain to hear him.

"What did they take from you?" Hilliard asked, suddenly very cold.

"Just some things that Gran brought for me. She sent things to try to help make sure I was as comfortable as possible. She also made sure I always had money in my account. But I never used it, because if I did, one of the men would take what I got. Thieves, bangers, addicts—everyone was in there. The guards were vigilant and did their best, but these guys didn't care half the time." He took a deep breath.

Hilliard didn't know what to say to that. He got the idea that Brian wasn't telling him everything, and he didn't blame him. He knew that he would talk when he was ready. For guys like Brian, their time behind bars was often like soldiers' time in combat. They didn't talk about it because it was something they didn't want to keep reliving, and it wasn't like most people could understand what they had been through. He took Brian's hand, still holding it as he checked out the window to make sure Timothy was truly gone.

"Don't let that ass take anything from you. Your great-aunt left you the house for a reason, and she cut him out of the will for one as well."

"Yeah. I know that." He really didn't like the idea of being here alone with Timothy out there. "It's just that when people get unreasonable and entitled, they tend to do stupid things, thinking they have some sort of right." Yet he knew that if Brian stayed, Beverly was going to be alone.

"Do you want me to stay?" Brian asked as if he were reading his mind.

"I'd like that, but doesn't Beverly need you?" He couldn't take Brian away in case she needed him.

"Gran will already be in bed." He pulled out his phone and made a call. "She says she's fine and will see me in the morning." Brian stepped closer, wrapping his arms around Hilliard's waist. "I know you have this 'go slow' thing in your head. But…."

Damn, Brian felt so good. Hilliard closed his eyes, just taking in the feel of Brian against him. He tried not to let memories of the last time he had felt this way come forward. It had been years, and…. He pushed thoughts of Alan away.

"The thing is, are you ready for something like what you're asking for?" Hilliard said, his eyes boring into Brian's. He wanted him and wasn't going to send him on his way. But there was something in his eyes—hesitation, worry perhaps—that gave Hilliard pause.

Brian looked away first. "I don't know." His gaze shifted to his feet.

"There's nothing to be ashamed of," Hilliard said softly.

"Of course there is," Brian retorted loudly. "I have plenty of reasons. People don't believe me. Some of them looked down on me when I was accused, and those same people now look down on me because I went to jail. It didn't matter that I did nothing wrong, and even if I could skywrite proof that I was innocent, they wouldn't believe it. They would continue to think that I'm the guy who robbed Violet and her family."

"But you didn't." Hilliard placed a hand on each shoulder. "And we can prove it. But we need to make sure our proof has impact and helps us catch the real thief. Everyone is going to know that they treated you badly." He intended to make sure of it.

"It isn't going to help. That can't take away what happened to me," Brian said softly.

Hilliard nodded. "No, it can't. No one can do that. I can try to make sure that the truth comes out. Only you can figure out how you live with the past. But know this: I will never hold it against you. Your past is just that—the past. What you have to do, what all of us need to do, is figure out how we are going to deal with it and then live with it." Hilliard paused, his shoulders slumping.

"What is it?"

"Alan," he said softly. "I know what shame is. See, I knew Alan had cheated, but I let it go. I thought that if I could make him happy, it would stop. I covered it up because I didn't want my friends to know. I figured that if I was more—if I was better and made him happier—then he would see what we originally had." He sighed, knowing he had been a complete fool. "I kept thinking that I was the cause and that I could fix it, but in the end it was his behavior, and I had to walk away." Hilliard shook his head hard as if to get the hurt and shame to empty out of it.

Brian tugged him into a hug, and Hilliard held Brian in return, the two of them comforting each other. They both needed to get past what had been done to them. Hilliard knew that what Alan had done wasn't of the magnitude of pain that Brian had been through, but this wasn't a contest about who hurt more, it was about trying to let the other begin to heal.

BRIAN HAD called his grandmother. Apparently she was already in bed with the dogs and, as Brian relayed, had told him not to worry about a thing. They each had a third beer, and then Hilliard turned off the lights and led the way to the bedroom, holding Brian's hand. "The bathroom is right there, and I put out an extra toothbrush and towels for you." He reluctantly released Brian's hand and went to his bedroom, leaving the door cracked open.

He got undressed and slipped into bed, waiting for Brian, who came inside. As much as he wanted to see Brian in all his glory, if only to see how his imagination measured up, Hilliard turned out the light.

Brian slipped under the covers, lying on his back, looking upward. "There's nothing to be worried about." Hilliard slipped his hand across Brian's chest, lying on his side. Then he held still.

"The last time someone touched me, it was…." He sighed deeply. "I turned to them and tossed them halfway across the room. I don't know where the strength came from, but I got him away from me. I hurt him, but no one messed with me again—at least not like that."

"Do I remind you of him?" Hilliard asked.

"No. You remind me of you. You are nothing like him." Brian put his hand on top of Hilliard's. "Nothing at all like him."

"Then go to sleep and try not to worry."

He sniffed. "Sometimes I have nightmares."

"We all do. Just different ones." Hilliard squeezed Brian's fingers and closed his eyes. "You get comfortable, and we'll keep the bad things at bay together." He eased away, and Brian rolled onto his side. Hilliard spooned against him, sharing Brian's warmth against the cool night air flowing in through the open window.

"I don't know if that's possible."

"Then we'll try," Hilliard told him in a whisper. It felt amazing to hold him, and he closed his eyes. Part of him knew he could easily get excited, but the nervousness of it being their first night together held him back. "I doubt I'll be able to sleep much tonight."

"Why?"

"Because I never sleep very well with someone else. Alan and I never really learned to sleep well in the same bed. After a year or so, he started leaving the bed in the night to sleep in the other room. Eventually we were only in the same bed when we had sex, and the rest of the time, we slept apart like one of those fifties television families. I should have known then that we weren't supposed to be together." He closed his eyes and listened to Brian's soft breathing and the sounds of the ocean from outside. As usual, it took him quite a while to fall to sleep, but eventually he gave way to exhaustion. Sleep finally settled over him. When he woke the following morning, he and Brian had switched places, with Brian holding him.

BRIAN WAS still asleep when Hilliard slipped out of bed and went downstairs to the kitchen. He put on the coffee maker and got out some things for a simple breakfast. He made toast and juice along with some fruit and placed it on a tray before returning to the bedroom.

"Brian," he said softly, loving the view with the covers askew and Brian lying with his perfect cotton-covered ass on display. He was a stunner, there was no doubt about that. He slowly rolled over and pulled up the covers. Hilliard had noticed his very attractive state but didn't mention it. He set the tray on Brian's lap and climbed into bed next to him. "It's pretty simple."

Brian lightly bumped Hilliard's shoulder and then kissed him. "I think this is the first time I've ever had breakfast in bed." They took their juice and slowly ate the toast. Hilliard fed Brian a strawberry, catching the juice as it ran over his lips.

"I never did anything like this before." He smiled and gently shifted closer to Brian. This was a great way to spend part of the morning, though he knew Brian would have to go to work pretty soon, and he had plenty to do himself. Still, it was nice to have a few minutes for just the two of them.

It took less time than Hilliard would have liked, but they finished their breakfast, and Brian shifted the tray before getting up. "I have a couple of jobs this morning that I have to finish, and I should make sure Gran is okay for the day." He pulled on his jeans and shrugged on his T-shirt, covering his lightly furred chest.

Hilliard set the tray aside. "You know, I think you should work shirtless. I bet you'd get more jobs… or at least people stopping to watch. I know I would." He leaned closer. "Just watching you is enough to make my heart race." He tugged Brian down and into a kiss that curled his toes.

"Me too," Brian whispered. "And I'd love nothing more than to stay here in bed with you and satisfy my own curiosity." He pressed Hilliard back down onto the mattress with his kiss, then climbed on and covered Hilliard with his clothed weight. Hilliard slipped his arm around his waist, holding Brian to him, loving his weight and solidity against him.

Hilliard was hard, his cock straining in his briefs. He was so damned tempted to strip Brian naked right now, but Brian pulled away and stepped back from the bed. "Damn, you make me want things I don't know if I have a right to." His hand shook as he took a step toward the door. "I have to go."

"Will I see you later?" Hilliard asked.

"Of course." Brian smiled and then left the room. Heavy footsteps followed on the stairs. The front door closed a minute later, and Hilliard wondered what Brian meant by "things I don't know if I have a right to." That was a strange turn of phrase, and Hilliard mulled it over until he got up to take a shower, because he and his imagination most definitely needed one.

HILLIARD SPENT the morning preparing for his exam. He had plenty of material to review, and he requested the appropriate paperwork from the Ohio Bar Association. Mainly he kept himself busy to stop himself from wondering about Brian.

He absently answered his phone as he sat at his laptop at the kitchen table, the doors open to catch the ocean breeze. "Hilliard, it's Beverly. I have a meeting with the church group this afternoon, and I was wondering if you'd like to go with me." The request took him a little by surprise. "These people know everyone, and if you're thinking of staying and opening a law practice, then you need to meet them."

"Okay, if you'd like me to go with you. What time is it?"

"They meet for lunch at the pub. We have a room that we use. It's just a social group. I don't normally go because it's hard to get around sometimes, but I will today."

"All right, I'll pick you up. Just let me know what time." She told him everything he needed to know.

"I'll plant a good seed today, and I'll be able to wipe the smug look off Violet's face that she's had for the last couple of years." She growled slightly.

"Remind me not to get on your bad side," he teased. "And remember, we need to unsettle her." A thought sent a chill up his spine. "One more thing. It's possible that Violet knows who the real thief is. Think about it."

"I worked that out already. And after the church meeting, I have an appointment with an old friend in the police department." Hilliard couldn't help thinking that he didn't want to be on the receiving end of Beverly's machinations. He got the feeling that the police and Violet wouldn't know what hit them.

"That's excellent. At the meeting, you spread the information, and I'll watch Violet." This could turn out to be interesting. "I'll see you then." He ended the call and had just gotten into his study material again when someone knocked on the door. Hilliard got up and went to answer it.

He opened it to Uncle Timothy and a man in a police uniform. "May I help you?" Hilliard asked, ignoring his uncle.

"It seems that you are inhabiting this house illegally. Timothy DuPrix says this is his mother's home and that you are residing here against his wishes."

Brian rolled his eyes. He should have expected something like this. Uncle Timothy was turning out to be more of a crackpot than he'd originally thought. "Actually, he's brought you here under false pretenses, and you might consider charges against him. His mother, my great-aunt Grace, passed away a few months ago and left me the house in her will. I have a copy of it. If you'd like to come inside, you may. But he is not to set foot in the house." He glared at Timothy.

"Now see here—"

"This is my property, no matter what you seem to think, and I don't want you inside." Hilliard crossed his arms over his chest, then turned to the officer. "Follow me." He let him inside and closed the door on his uncle, locking it because he didn't trust him. Then Hilliard asked the officer to wait and went upstairs. He went to the room that would one day be his office once he'd found some proper furnishings. He got his copy of the will, opening it to the appropriate page as he descended the stairs once more. "As you can see from this document, I inherited the house, and Uncle Timothy received a grand total of ten dollars. Apparently his mother didn't think very much of her 'useless and greedy' son."

"I see." The officer turned to where Timothy glared through the window.

"Do you?" Hilliard asked. "He brought you here under false circumstances so he could try to intimidate me and get you involved in illegal activity. This is harassment, and he involved the police." He smiled. "I suspect you'll know exactly how the handle this situation."

"Yes, I do, and I thank you for your help." The officer turned, his belt creaking a little as he went to the door. Hilliard unlocked it, and the officer stepped outside.

"That will is a fake and—" Uncle Timothy immediately sputtered.

"That would be for someone other than me to decide. But as far as I can tell, it looked correct." He paused on the steps. "You are lucky that neither he nor I are pressing charges, because we both could. I have real work to attend to, and I will wait to make sure you leave town. And I suggest you don't bother this man again. Understood? We will not be as forgiving the next time." Hilliard closed the door and let the officer handle his duty while he went back to work.

WHEN HILLIARD pulled up later that morning, Gran was waiting out in front with the dogs on leashes. "Are they coming as well?"

Beverly nodded. "If it's okay. Poppy and Gigi love it there. They have treats for them, and they'll lie under the table while we eat."

"Of course," he said and helped her down the walk and into the car. The dogs jumped right into the back and settled down. It was a little misty, so he'd kept the top up. Once he got in, he drove downtown, where he was able to find a parking space right in front of the restaurant. Gran climbed out and led the dogs inside, with Hilliard following her through to the tent-covered garden area that had been closed off with the seating rearranged so everyone would be close.

"Beverly," one of the ladies called as she hugged her. "It's been a while." They all seemed glad to see her, and Hilliard stayed out of the way.

"This is my new friend and neighbor, Hilliard. He inherited the house from Grace and has been helping both Brian and myself." Hilliard shook hands with each of the ladies as they introduced themselves in quick enough succession that he was never going to be able to keep their names straight. The only one he was interested in was Violet, who approached last.

"It's good of you to come," Violet said coolly before turning to Hilliard with an expression of warning. When he ignored it, she turned back to Beverly. "How is your grandson doing since…?" Violet left the remaining part of her question open.

"Actually, very well, especially after the past few days." Beverly sat down, the dogs lying at her feet while the other ladies gathered around. It seemed she hadn't joined the group in a while, so she was the center of attention. "Brian and I took a trip up the coast with Hilliard this past weekend. He has the most amazing convertible, and I had such fun. We stopped at the Cabrillo Point lighthouse. It was really nice."

"I volunteer there part-time, you know," one of the ladies said. "It's pretty wonderful to climb up to the light and get a look up and down the coast."

"Maybe I'll see if Brian and Hilliard would like to do that. I can't anymore, but I'm sure it is a sight." Her smile was perfection, and she had the ladies captivated. "But we found out something amazing. Carol, did you know they had security cameras?"

"Yes. I see them when I volunteer."

"And they never aged out the files! We asked when we were there, and they were able to find Chester and Brian on their tapes." She turned to Violet. "On the very day that poor Violet was robbed—and right in the middle of the time she says it happened!"

All the ladies gasped, but Violet's expression seemed carved in stone. "You don't mean…?"

"I do. It's proof that he was innocent all along and that the real thief is still out there. Hilliard is helping us find an attorney so we can petition to have his conviction overturned, and I'm meeting with the police this afternoon to let them know that the real thief is still at large and that they should be looking for them. Isn't that great news? I've always believed in him, you know."

"Of course you did," one of the ladies said before hugging her. "We've been praying for something like this for a long time." Carol was clearly happy for Beverly, and so were most of the others.

Violet looked as if she had sucked a lemon. "That doesn't prove anything."

"Actually, it proves nearly everything. They were there for at least an hour, from before one until nearly two, and then they went to lunch." Beverly's tone remained light, but there was steel in her voice. Beverly was exaggerating the times a little, but it seemed to be having the desired effect.

"Isn't that great, Violet?" one of the ladies asked, her expression fading when Violet scowled and headed toward the exit.

"Where are you going?" Beverly asked, making sure to draw everyone's attention. She was sneaky, that was for sure.

"Just out to my car," she said. Hilliard met Beverly's gaze and went inside toward the bathrooms, right through the crowded restaurant and out toward where Violet was on the phone.

"Apparently they have found something that proves Brian didn't commit the burglary," she said as she stood near her car. Hilliard went around the back of the vehicles and got close enough to hear better. "I don't know what we should do. Beverly says they can prove he was not here in town, and that means…." She shook her head and sighed. "What the heck are we going to do? The police might investigate once more, but who knows? If Beverly gives what she has to them and starts putting on pressure…." She turned away, and it was harder for Hilliard to hear what she was saying.

Damn, that sure seemed like a guilty phone call. Was she warning someone? He wished he knew who was on the other end of that call. Still, it was something to go on and meant that he definitely needed to pay her a visit. Hilliard backed away and returned the way he had come, sitting down with Beverly as Violet returned. He pasted on his most innocent smile and leaned to Beverly. "I want to get a look at her phone if it's possible. She made a call, and I want to know who it was."

"No problem," Beverly told him. "Violet, there's a seat over here. My dogs always just love you." She was pouring it on thick, that was for certain.

The other tables were full, so Violet took the seat next to Hilliard, across from Beverly, and the dogs did their part, approaching her for pets. She set her phone on the table, and fortunately Hilliard didn't have to do anything as a few messages came in. He was able to see the name Frank on them and suspected they were from whoever she had called. He couldn't see the messages, but a name was as good as anything else.

"It's good to see you again," he told Violet before picking up his menu to look it over.

"We don't usually bring guests to these sorts of things," Violet said flatly.

Cindy sat down on Hilliard's left side. "Of course we do. Everyone is welcome, you know that."

"Well," Hilliard began, "Beverly needed a ride since Brian is working, and I had a little time between my work studying for the state bar exam. I haven't decided quite what I'm going to do long-term, but I know that being licensed to practice here is only going to help my career." He smiled and took a drink of his water, watching Violet as she seemed to look over the rest of the room. "Is there someone you're looking for? I can check out front for you."

"No," she answered quickly. "I was hoping that someone was going to be here, but they didn't seem to make it."

That was a bald-faced lie, but Hilliard didn't call her on it. Violet was terrible at fibbing, and the more she spoke, the more she gave away. "That's okay. You and Beverly must be old friends, and it has to be a huge relief to know that her grandson wasn't the person who broke into your family home after all." He laid it on thick, but Violet didn't seem to be paying attention.

"Yes, that's true. Violet and I have been friends for years, and events put a strain on things, but now we can hopefully start again," Beverly said. "Isn't that right?"

"Of course," Violet said absently.

Beverly didn't press it either, and Hilliard shared a smile with her as he went ahead and ordered lunch. He wished Brian were here to watch Violet squirm like a fish on a hook.

Chapter 10

BRIAN WAS exhausted. Every project he took on today seemed fraught with issues. First there wasn't enough drywall compound to patch a hole in Mrs. Grant's ceiling, and then the pipe he'd gotten to fix Mr. Fox's sink wasn't exactly right. He knew he should be grateful for the work, but by the time he got back to Gran's and dragged himself inside, he could barely walk.

"I made you some dinner," Gran said. "Your plate is in the oven."

"Thanks, Gran," he said softly. "I'm going to eat and go right up to bed."

Gran chuckled. "I don't think so. Your Hilliard and I had a nice lunch today with the church ladies. He got some interesting insight into Violet, but we didn't get to talk about it afterwards. I needed to lie down, and he had work to do. So I picked up some sweets at the store, and he'll be here in half an hour. I figured you'd want to hear what he thought. So sit down and eat your dinner. Then go upstairs, clean up, and be ready when he gets here." She adjusted the blanket over her legs and patted her lap. Both dogs jumped up and made themselves at home.

Brian knew better than to argue with Gran, so he went to have his dinner before taking a shower. By the time he came back downstairs, Gran and Hilliard were sitting together in the living room with cups of tea, another waiting for him on the coffee table.

"What's going on? Why do I feel like this is the Spanish Inquisition?" He squirmed at the way they both looked at him, and he had to remind himself he wasn't a naughty child.

"It's not," Hilliard said. "But I think Violet couldn't get out of that restaurant fast enough after lunch."

"I don't think I've seen that woman move that quickly in years, the gossipy old biddy."

Brian couldn't help chuckling. "So what happened?"

"Your Gran laid it on thick. It was beautiful. The other ladies at the luncheon were thrilled to see her and immediately thought her news was wonderful. Violet just paled and then hurried outside to make a phone call. I managed to hear part of it, but I'm not sure if she knows who is behind the burglary. She said some things that are suspicious, but it could also mean that the case will be reopened and that everything will start again."

"Who was she talking to?" Brian asked.

"I'm not sure. She didn't say a name, but I did get a peek at her phone, and she was getting text messages from a Frank."

"Her son," Beverly supplied. "She has two, Frank and Ansen. Frank is the one she's closest to, while Ansen lives on the East Coast somewhere and rarely comes home. I think he couldn't get away from her fast enough."

"Okay, so she was talking to her son after getting troubling news. Is that so suspicious?" Brian asked. "If Gran were in her place, she'd probably call me and tell me about it." He didn't really see where this got him anything other than maybe running in circles. "You know, we aren't detectives, so maybe we should leave this to the police. Turn everything over to them and let them figure out who really pulled off the burglary. We can prove it wasn't me. That will help me get my life back and…."

Gran leaned forward a little, her face hardening. Brian knew that was the wrong thing to say. "That tape only means that it is *unlikely* that you were the thief. It doesn't rule you out completely. Though people would be stupid to think otherwise, it's still ridiculously possible." She huffed.

"Okay, Gran," he said gently. "Please don't get yourself upset."

"I'm just making sure you understand that we aren't at the finish line yet." She sat back, and Hilliard sipped his tea, tension in the room lingering.

Brian huffed. "Do you know how much I hate this?" he asked softly. "It seems like every waking moment is spent consumed by this stupid burglary and me. Both of you are spending all this energy trying to prove a negative, which is nearly impossible. I didn't break into that house, someone else did. The court said that I did, and now we are turning in circles to try to prove I didn't. I just wish I could live my life without all this." He took Gran's hand. "I want you to be able to spend your time enjoying life and being happy. Hell, I want to be happy too. But this whole thing hangs over me all the damned time. And now I feel like I'm dragging you into it as well."

"That's enough of that nonsense," Gran told him. "We're doing this because we care."

Hilliard nodded and put an arm around his shoulder. "Your Gran loves you, and she wants you to be happy. You shouldn't have been put in this position in the first place. It wasn't right." He paused. "Look, this is important to me now. And you aren't putting either of us out. We want to help, okay?" Brian's skin tingled as Hilliard ran his fingers along his jawline.

Brian wondered just when Hilliard and Gran had gotten close enough that he was speaking for her. But Gran simply nodded and put her feet down. The dogs whined before jumping down and going to the bed in the corner, where they curled up together.

A knock sounded, and Gran went to the door and opened it. "I saw your lights," Gran said as she stepped back to let an older man come inside. He had close-cut white hair and intense blue eyes. On this man, the normal signs of aging seemed to make him more distinguished and handsome.

Brian stood, along with Hilliard.

"Boys, this is Grant Whittaker. He's with the Mendocino County Sheriff's Office." She smiled and led him inside. "Grant, this is my grandson, Brian, and his friend Hilliard." She swallowed. "That is the right term, isn't it?" she asked.

"It's fine for now." Hilliard placed his hand at the small of Brian's back, his touch gentle and reassuring. "It's good to meet you." Hilliard shook Grant's hand. "Just so you know, I have been acting as a friend to both Beverly and Brian. I am an attorney in Ohio, but not here in California."

"I see," Grant said. "A lawyerly answer and a good one." He smiled. "I understand the desire to help. Thank you." He handed Brian a folder. "Beverly asked me for a copy of the police file on your case. Since the case is officially closed, it's part of the public record."

"Shall we go to the table?" Gran offered, and they all sat at the kitchen table.

Brian opened the file and looked over the front page.

"May I?" Hilliard asked, leaving Brian to read while he took the rest of the file. "Okay. Take a look at this. Here's Violet's statement. She says she left the house at twelve thirty for her meeting at the church and got home at a little before three, when she discovered the burglary had taken place." He pulled out a tablet and made notes. "That narrows down the timeline even more."

"May I see that?" Grant asked.

"We found video footage of Brian and his grandfather visiting the light station on the day of the burglary. I added the times from the tape."

Grant shook his head. "Jesus," he whispered. "And they never bothered to check earlier?" He blinked. "They never would have been able to bring charges if they'd had this."

"I figured that. But the burden of proof is much higher now that Brian has been convicted. Reasonable doubt isn't enough any longer. I'm not licensed here, but I did my research, and the best way to prove his innocence is still to find the real thief."

Grant pulled the file to him and flipped through the pages. "Here are the suspects that the investigators were initially looking at. Kevin and Kendall Trainer, as well as Michael Rogers and Nathan West. It's well known that those four are thick as thieves and definite troublemakers. They have all had minor run-ins with the law over the years."

"Tell me about it," Brian said between clenched teeth.

"Anyway, the department had asked all of them to provide alibis, and they seemed to be having trouble explaining their whereabouts. Evidently the investigators were looking pretty closely at them until we received an anonymous tip, and then one of the stolen pieces was found in your truck with your fingerprints on it."

"And that was that," Brian muttered. "They asked me for an alibi, and all I had was a day away with Gramps, who was dead, and I was on the hook."

"I have to tell you that any decent lawyer should have been able to put the pieces together that you were framed. Looking at it, I would have gone so much further."

"Grant joined the department a little over a year ago after he retired from the LAPD and moved up here." Gran smiled, and if Brian didn't know better, he'd have said that she had a thing for the police officer.

"So what do we do?" Brian asked.

Gran added, "Can you help us?"

"Yes, I think this was botched from the get-go, and it needs to be made right. Can I get a copy of the video, as well as the timeline you put together? I want to do some more work and see what else I can dig up. The officer who headed this investigation isn't with the department any longer, so I doubt I'm going to meet with resistance. But still, I want to get approval."

Brian nodded, relieved that more people were beginning to believe in him. Hilliard once again put an arm around his shoulder, and Brian leaned into the touch.

"At least you have the support you deserve," Hilliard said softly.

"I know, but where do we go from here?" Brian asked. "I mean, do we have to get a court to declare that I was wrongly convicted?" That could take forever.

"Yes. But if we can get rock-solid proof, then I can take it to the police department as well as the prosecutor's office. They can help you move this through the courts. Petitions like ours take a while through the normal processes, but if the prosecutor goes with us before a judge with a proper writ and asks that their original verdict be vacated, then that can be a much faster route. Justice can be slow, but I like to think it will happen in the end." Grant wasn't particularly encouraging.

"Look, what we can do is get the proof, and then we can get the local media to pick up the story. Once they see the proof, then everyone is going to know that you were wrongly convicted. This is about the town knowing you aren't the thief as much as anything else." Hilliard held Brian's hand tightly. "So please don't worry about it."

"He's right," Grant said softly. "And I think that we could be getting close."

"So what do we do from here?" Brian asked.

Grant huffed. "You know my official answer would be to let the police do their work, but considering the fact that we didn't do that the first time around, I'm going to say this: everyone you talk to could be the thief, and you have no idea how desperate they may be. They broke into your truck to plant evidence the first time." His expression was stone-cold serious. "They have spent the past almost three years thinking they got away with it. The thief has gone on with their life, likely cashed in their ill-gotten gains, and maybe used it to build the foundation of their life. Now all that is threatened. The snake is most dangerous when it's been backed into a corner." He gathered the report and put it back together. "Just remember to be careful."

"I know. If we stir up a hornet's nest, expect to get stung," Hilliard said. "But if we don't do a little stirring, we might never get to the bottom of this."

Grant nodded. "But think about this. Right now, we have proof that casts great doubt on Brian's conviction. He is home and rebuilding his life. Beverly is doing well, and…." He smiled. "It seems to me that things are going well on all fronts. Going around nest-stirring could jeopardize all of that." He picked up the file.

"Is it possible for you to leave that with us?" Hillard asked.

Grant set it back on the table. "It's a copy, but don't flash around that you have it." He said good night and left the house.

Brian leaned against Hilliard's shoulder. "Where do we go from here?"

Gran grinned. "Let's talk to people and see if we can puzzle this thing out. Eat your heart out, Jessica Fletcher." And danged if he and Hilliard didn't both laugh.

Brian wasn't sure about this, but he and Hilliard stood outside the scene of the crime, staring at the large Victorian-era home that had been an anchor of the town, competing in prominence with the Masonic Hall for over a century. "I don't know if this is a good idea or not."

"She doesn't have to speak with us, and she might not. But I get the feeling that she knows more than she's saying and that she is going to be damned curious what we have. For her, the nightmare has been over. The person who victimized her has been punished, and now that's being ripped away. I want to see how she reacts and try to figure out what she knows." Hilliard gave Brian a hint of heat in his smile, which sent a shiver through him as he remembered last night, and the way Hilliard transported him to a place where he forgot about everything other than Hilliard's mouth and the way he used it to send Brian into ecstasy. "You don't have to come."

He didn't want to, but he was too curious to go back to Gran's and wait, so he followed Hilliard up the walk to the front door, which opened before Hilliard knocked.

"I saw you coming." Violet's cold eyes swept over him, and Brian did his best to pretend he hadn't seen it. "What is it you want?" The light dress she wore would have been more appropriate for a garden party than just sitting in her house, and Brian wondered if they were keeping her from something.

"I know what Beverly told you at lunch the other day, and, well… we know how difficult this is for you."

Her gaze narrowed. "You think you do?" she asked.

Hilliard nodded gently. "Yes. You were the victim, not the enemy. You were the one who was initially hurt in all this. Having things taken from your home also robs you of your sense of safety. We know that, and we aren't here to cause you any more pain."

"That's a real nice speech, but what is it you want?" Violet asked.

Hilliard kept his cool. "Believe it or not, we're on the same side. Brian wasn't the person who broke into your house. He was with his grandfather, just as we said, and we can prove that. The evidence from his truck was planted, which means that the real thief is still out there, and we all have an interest in finding them and maybe getting your things back." Damn, Hilliard really was a great lawyer and amazing with words.

Brian didn't move, and Violet seemed torn with indecision. "I don't know what I can do to help you, but I suppose you should come in rather than standing out here where everyone in town can see you and wonder what's going on." She stepped back, and they went inside.

Brian expected "fussy old lady" style when he stepped inside, but he was surprised at how large and weighty the furniture was. Not that it didn't feel right, just that it was imposing and impressive, and somehow reflected Violet at the same time—and that was just the hall. The living room where she led them was equally impressive. She motioned them to chairs, and Brian perched on the edge of the seat, extremely uncomfortable.

"I suppose you're here to try to convince me or something," Violet said.

Hilliard shook his head. "I don't think I need to convince you, because you already knew—or at least suspected—that Brian was never the thief." He came right out with it. "When you first came home and discovered the burglary, who did you think had broken in?"

"I don't think that has any bearing on this," she retorted, her back straight, eyes intense as ever.

"Oh, I think it does. I know that you had the house on a home tour a few months before the burglary, but Beverly tells me that most of the portable valuables had been put away. Yet as far as I can gather, that was the reasoning behind why someone would know what to take."

"That's true. I figured that they snooped around when no one was in the rooms…." She was grasping at straws.

"Weren't there docents?" Brian asked gently, and Violet eventually nodded.

"It was what the police thought as well." As though that justified her position.

"I understand, but who might actually know where the stolen items were kept? Some of them weren't items that you would keep sitting out, were they?"

"What do you take me for? A fool?" Violet stood. "Of course not. I'm not going to leave a collection of antique sterling just lying about. It was put away and…." She sat back down, paling. "But the police said that they found one of the pieces, so that…." Violet turned to him, her eyes softening. "Can you really prove it wasn't you?"

Brian nodded. "I spent the day with Gramps, and we have proof that he and I were together, as I said all along."

Violet lowered her head. "So my nightmare isn't over." She wrapped the shawl from the back of the chair around her shoulders. "Have the police seen what you have?"

"Yes, they have. We are developing a case to have the conviction vacated. But I'm afraid none of this is going to be over until the real thieves are found." Hilliard's voice was so gentle. "And that's why we're asking for your help. If you have any ideas about who it might be, then maybe we can put this behind us all forever."

Violet pulled the shawl closer around her. "I wish I knew."

Brian found himself watching her and then glanced at Hilliard, who seemed almost comfortable sitting back in the stiff chair. There was something about him, a presence that didn't seem to get flustered. It helped give Brian confidence of a sort. If anyone could sort through this mess, it was Hilliard.

"I have to ask. Are you acting as Brian's lawyer?"

Hilliard shook his head. "No. I'm not a member of the California bar. I'm acting as his friend. Nothing more." He leaned in, those intense eyes that looked deep into Brian's when they were alone drawing Violet closer. "I just hate to see miscarriages of justice. I know mistakes happen, we all make them, but this is one we can right. And we need your help. You don't have to give it, of course, but I want to see if we can get back what was taken from you." He blinked. "I know some of what was taken you can never get back." That voice wrapped around Brian like a blanket, and he could see it having the same effect on Violet.

She sighed and seemed to come to a decision. "Okay. Assuming that Brian isn't the thief—and I'm not saying that I buy all of what you're selling, but let's say he isn't—then where do we go from here?" Her eyes still held skepticism, but also a little of the lady that Brian knew from when he trick-or-treated at this house and Violet dressed as her namesake from Willy Wonka, covered in blue makeup.

"Who might have known what you had? It was an antique necklace that was found in Brian's truck. Did you keep that out? Or in a jewelry box?"

Violet shook her head. "That's the tough thing. I kept it at the bottom of a drawer in my bedroom. The jewelry box was on my dresser, but they stole that piece of jewelry from the drawer."

Hilliard leaned closer. "Was the entire room tossed?" Violet looked confused. "Did the thieves ransack the room?"

"Oh… no. When I noticed the silver was gone, I hurried up here to find the cloth bag I kept my jewelry in, and it was gone."

Hilliard pulled out a small tablet from his pocket and began making a few notes. "What else was taken?" He already knew from the police report, but Brian supposed he was trying to keep her talking.

"I made a list for the police, but later…." She got up and opened a case behind her chair. Then she pointed. "There were a couple of Japanese netsukes that my father brought back from a trip there. I didn't recognize they were gone until months later." The pain in her eyes was palpable.

"Do you have pictures of them somewhere?" Brian asked.

Violet pulled out her iPhone, then shook her head. "Yes, I do. They're on the computer in the office, though. Frank said that I should make an inventory of the things in the house for insurance purposes. He and I were taking pictures of them."

"Why didn't you report them missing?"

Violet shrugged. "I figured they were gone like the rest of it. You were already paying for the crime, and I didn't think any good would come of it. So I sort of wrote them off."

"I suppose it happens a lot." Brian cleared his throat. "But I want you to know that I never stole anything from anyone. I've worked hard all my life, and I was accused at the same time as I lost my grandfather." A lump grew in his throat, and he gave up trying to finish what he meant to say.

"That was a bad time for all of us," Violet said gently.

"Then let's try to put it behind us, find out what truly happened, and then maybe everyone—both of you in particular—can have some peace… knowing the truth."

Violet nodded slowly. "Yes. I think that's best." She stood, and Brian did as well, with Hilliard following. She led them to the door, and Brian thanked her before leaving the house. Violet closed the door almost silently after them, and they went down the walk to the street.

"That was interesting," Brian said. "And weird at the same time."

"It was more than that."

"How do you figure?"

Hilliard led the way down the street as they headed toward his house. "Violet doesn't know who robbed her, but she's still afraid. Afraid that someone will do it again, and with you being innocent, she's afraid of who it might be. Her son knew what she had and helped her inventory it. Her grandsons knew what was there. The one thing that is for sure—it was someone who knew her pretty well. They went into her room and got her jewelry without ransacking everything. That means they knew where she hid it. That was the thief's mistake and something more the police should have been able to figure out."

"But they only had me in their sights," Brian said. "And after that, they didn't look any further."

"The thing is, *we* have to. And we need to tell Grant what we found," Hilliard explained. "It isn't going to be long before the guilty party is put on notice, and they will be looking to cast all eyes in another direction. After all, it worked well before."

"What do you suggest I do? I have to work."

"Of course you do, and you can't put your life on hold, but make sure everything is locked, and like I said before, watch those around you."

"I added cameras to my truck, both inside and out. So if someone does try to frame me the way they did before, we'll know who it is."

"Good, though this time they'll be sneakier." Hilliard took his hand. "But we'll be ready for them. You aren't alone, and you have people who believe in you." That was something Brian had wondered if he'd ever have again.

Chapter 11

THE FOLLOWING evening, Hilliard checked himself in the mirror for the third time and turned away. He looked fine and was acting like a nervous teenager hoping to lose his virginity on prom night simply because he didn't want to mess this up. He closed the closet door and went downstairs. He and Brian were having a proper date, which meant he was picking Brian up and they were going to the Ledford House for dinner rather than eating in town at the pub… again. He checked the time, grabbed the flowers he'd gotten that afternoon, hurried outside to the Mustang, and lowered the top.

He drove slowly through town, waving to people he knew. It was so strange, but this tiny place on the edge of the Pacific was quickly beginning to feel like home. He had memories here, and it was a chance for him to start over. Yes, Cleveland had been his home for most of his life, and he had intended to build something he could be proud of there, but all that had changed. Almost everything in his life had changed over the past few months, and maybe that was a good thing.

The lights were on at Beverly's. It wasn't that late, but the marine layer had moved in, casting the town in a moody pall that always made Hilliard wonder if something was about to happen. He got out, strode up to the door, and knocked softly, the dogs barking on the other side.

Brian opened the door, keeping the dogs back as Hilliard stepped inside. "You look nice," Hilliard told Brian. He expected a smile, but what he got was fear. Hilliard glanced to Beverly, whose expression was stormy. "What happened?" He handed the small bouquet to Beverly.

"I better show you," Brian said before leading Hilliard through the house and up the stairs. "I worked all day, and when I got home, I came up here to change clothes. When I opened my sock drawer…." He went to his room and pulled the top drawer of the dresser back. Sitting in the corner was a silver wing, part of something, poking out from next to a pair of rolled-up gray socks. "What do I do?"

"Have Gran call Grant right now." Hilliard had been afraid of something like this. They were casting doubt on the status quo, and that had made someone pretty scared.

"She already did. He's on his way over."

"Then touch nothing. I'm assuming that you were in here this morning and there was no little silver angel thing in the drawer at that time." He already knew the answer. "Go sit with your grandmother and let me have a look around. Just leave the drawer open and come with me." He was pissed as all hell. Hilliard went to the front door as Brian sat with Beverly in the living room. He checked to see if it had been jimmied but found no sign of that. He was heading to the back when he heard a knock out front and let Grant inside.

"What happened?" Grant asked, dressed in his uniform.

"Our little evidence planter is at it again. Brian found it when he was getting dressed. Go on up—we left the drawer open." Hilliard followed him up and showed him what turned out to be an angel-decorated silver napkin ring, obviously part of Violet's missing set. "It wasn't here this morning when Brian dressed, so it must have been planted sometime today." He was going to insert the version of the story that he wanted to keep at the forefront in Grant's mind.

"Okay…." Grant turned skeptically.

Hilliard rolled his eyes. "Please. I saw the report, and so did you. The police executed a search warrant on this house at the time he was arrested. Are you saying they didn't look in his sock drawer? And like he was going to move evidence to incriminate himself just when we have the proof that he never perpetrated the burglary in the first place." He put his hands on his hips.

"I believe you," Grant said, making a placating gesture. "This is a frame-up if ever I saw one." He pulled on a pair of gloves and put the silver bauble into an evidence bag.

"Don't be surprised if you find a print on it. That seems to be their MO." Hilliard didn't like this at all.

"I know." Grant took a few photographs and left the room. He checked the front door and then the back, smiling when he found a few wood scrapings. "This is how they got in. Used a small screwdriver to jimmy the lock. You can see the scrapings if you look closely enough." He made notes before going in to speak with Beverly and Brian. He went over where Brian was all day and got a detailed account.

Beverly said, "I went to the church for a few hours this afternoon for a meeting. My ladies' group is working on school sets for needy children for the fall, and I was there helping to fill backpacks. It's something we do every year."

"Which explains when they got in," Hilliard said. "But not who is doing this." He could tell that Brian was as anxious as anything. "Brian and I were supposed to go out tonight," he explained when he noticed how Grant kept looking at each of them. He doubted that Brian would be up for it and excused himself to call the restaurant to let them know that something had come up. When he returned, Grant was still speaking with Brian. "What else do you need?"

"Nothing, actually." Grant headed for the front door and paused. "Actually, something just occurred to me."

Hilliard snorted. "The Columbo routine doesn't look good on you."

Grant grinned. "Why now?"

"That's easy. We went to see Violet yesterday, and I think she understands that Brian isn't the thief. We were asking her who might have known where some of the items were located, since none of it had been on public display since the house tour. And her jewelry would take someone time to find."

"You think this was an inside job."

"Aren't most of them? Burglars aren't going to break into a house that doesn't have anything easy to steal, and if they do, they take televisions and electronics. They certainly aren't going to go rummaging through drawers and stuff to find things, and if they do, they are going to leave a mess. According to Violet, there was no mess. Something else the police missed originally." Hilliard was glad the original investigator was no longer on the case, though an idea tickled the back of his mind. Something was just too far off. Yes, the police made mistakes, but he doubted that anyone was this stupid. There had to be more to it.

"All right. I have to say for the record that I'm not in favor of what you're doing." Grant's eyes were hard.

"These boys are shaking the trees, and the fruit is falling," Beverly replied.

"All we're doing is talking to people." And someone's name just moved up on the list, but that could wait until the current drama had passed. "If there's no more questions?' Hilliard said, letting Grant out and closing the door.

"Well, that was not the evening I was expecting. But Grant is convinced that someone broke in and planted evidence while you were at your church meeting. Why they kept the pieces all this time I have no idea. And whoever they are, they're getting more and more jumpy."

"So we back off and let things die down?" Brian said hopefully.

Hilliard shook his head and opened his mouth, but Beverly beat him to it. "We shake the trees harder and scare the ever-loving crap out of them," she said with a grin, taking Brian's hand. "We need to bring this to a close and let you get your life back."

"We're close, I can feel it. Just a few more facts and the picture should become clear. Then we can give what we have to Grant and let him bring this to an end." Hilliard sat down and tugged Brian onto the chintz sofa next to him. "Right now, you need to relax. This is progress, and more evidence than we had before. The only person we spoke with was Violet, and that was yesterday."

"True, but she could have spoken to half the town by now."

"No, she couldn't. Violet came down with the flu. She has been sick since right after you spoke with her and wasn't at church today."

Hilliard nodded and tugged Brian against him, listening as he sighed softly. "There will be time to figure this whole thing out." Right now, he needed to make Brian feel better, and he knew just how to do it. "Will you be okay here for a few hours?" he asked Beverly softly.

"Of course," she whispered, and Hilliard took Brian by the hand and led him outside. He waited while Brian locked the door and then got him in the car and made the return drive home. This hadn't been how he had seen the evening going, but he intended to make sure Brian got what he needed.

"WHAT ARE we doing?" Brian asked once Hilliard had fed them each a microwave dinner. Maybe in the future he could see if Brian's grandmother would be willing to cook for him and he could put meals in the freezer or something.

Hilliard finished stacking the dishes in the sink. "I had planned on taking you out for a nice dinner and then back here to watch a movie. I thought we could ignore whatever we were watching and make out like teenagers, but things have changed." He rinsed the dishes a bit before turning off the water. "I need to get some things." Hilliard approached

Brian and stood behind his chair, slipping his arms over his shoulders, then running his hands down his chest. "Go on upstairs and get undressed, then lie down on my bed. I'll be up in just a few minutes." He kissed the top of Brian's head.

Brian hesitated and then stood to walk into the front room and up the stairs, his shoulders carrying so much tension that Hilliard was afraid Brian's muscles might explode. He went into the downstairs bathroom and rummaged in a box he'd stashed under the sink. He'd meant to unpack it but had just left it there and… yes… just what he was looking for.

Hilliard grabbed what he needed. He checked that the doors were locked and headed upstairs, turning out the lights as he went. When he approached his bedroom, he stepped in and stopped. Brian lay on his belly, naked, the sight stopping Hilliard for a few seconds. The man was stunning, wide shoulders tapering to a narrow waist, and an ass that could crack walnuts. Hilliard swallowed hard before setting the bottle beside the bed and then slipping out of his clothes.

Slowly, he climbed onto the bed, grabbed the small bottle of lightly scented oil, rubbed some in his hands, and touched Brian's shoulders before beginning a slow, gentle massage.

Brian's skin was smooth and hot under his hands as he ran them over his back, the oil slicking the way. "Is this helping?" he asked, and received a deep, long groan before settling his weight across Brian's legs. He continued stroking slowly, shifting his weight with each long movement, up over his shoulders, down his back, and then up across his firm bubble butt. He didn't make any sort of sexual advance. This time right now was just to try to help Brian let go of some of his tension. The rest could wait for a while.

"Where did you learn to do this?" Brian asked, his voice deep and rumbly.

"My undergrad roommate was working on physical therapy, and he needed to practice. So I was a willing subject on a lot of evenings when the tension became almost unbearable." He ran his hands along Brian's sides and down to the tops of his legs before continuing upward once more. This time he concentrated on his shoulders, keeping his touch light. He wasn't qualified for deep tissue massage, and the last thing he wanted to do was hurt Brian. But he knew there was something almost magical in someone else's touch. "Is that helping?"

"Yeah," Brian whispered as Hilliard felt some of the anxiety slip away. Brian didn't move, his breathing becoming deeper and more regular. That was a good sign. Hilliard didn't need him to talk, just lie there and let Hilliard try to help him.

"Then just relax."

"I'm trying, but not all of me is cooperating."

Hilliard smiled. "Just ignore that part, close your eyes, and breathe deeply." He continued his slow massage before scooting down and having Brian roll over. "I see. That's pretty unignorable." Hilliard left Brian's cock alone and worked on his chest and arms. "All you need to do is breathe." He knew he was reminding him over and over, but with each exhalation, Brian grew more and more pliant. "That's it." He continued downward, massaging Brian's legs and feet until he closed his eyes. All tension seemed to have left him, which was exactly what Hilliard was trying for. There was only so much anxiety a person could take, and letting go of it was often hard.

"Is that it?" Brian asked, half mumbling, like he was partially asleep.

"Yes. Just relax. There's nothing you need to worry about."

Brian opened his eyes. "There's plenty to worry about, but not tonight."

Hilliard leaned closer. "Remember that you aren't alone. Not like last time. There are people who believe in you and who will ensure that the truth comes out. But for now, that can all wait." He lay down next to him. "Keep your eyes closed and breathe as deeply as you can. There is nothing to worry about here. There's only me and you." He kissed him gently, letting Brian know that it was that simple.

"Okay," he breathed, and kept his eyes closed. Hilliard lay still, his head on Brian's chest, and listened to the beat of his heart.

HILLIARD YAWNED and slipped under the covers as the air chilled around them.

"Do you always keep the window open?" Brian asked.

"Uh-huh," Hilliard hummed. "This time of year it is stiflingly hot in Cleveland, sometimes near a hundred degrees. I like the fact that the evenings are cool here and that I can sleep at night." He pulled the covers up over both of them. "I don't need air-conditioning."

"I know. It's the height of summer, and ten miles inland it's in the nineties right now. But here it's cool." He snuggled closer, and Hilliard wrapped his arms around Brian, drawing him in. Their lips met in the darkness, and the sea air blowing in through the window couldn't stop the building heat between them. "You feel so good."

Hilliard ran his hands down Brian's strong back and over his ass, cupping his cheeks, pressing the two of them together. "This day was so different from what I expected."

"I'm sorry," Brian whispered.

"Don't be. I wanted to take you to dinner and then bring you back here. Have a nice evening and then bring you up here to bed. Things took a different turn, but I'm right here with you, where I want to be." He smiled, even though it was dark. "We just had a slight bump in the road." He rolled Brian back on the bed and pressed him into the mattress.

"Yeah, but what happens when the bump turns into a pothole big enough to lose a car in?" Brian sighed. "It's happened before."

"I know." Hilliard kissed him and then held Brian as he rolled onto his side. It didn't seem like things were going to work out the way he thought, and that was fine. A lot had happened, and maybe sex right now wasn't the best idea. Being together and supporting Brian, that was what mattered at the moment. "Try to go to sleep and we'll deal with everything in the morning." He hoped both of them got some rest.

A KNOCKING woke him at… Hilliard glanced at the clock next to the bed. He pushed back the covers and got out as the sound came again. He climbed out of bed, pulled on his robe, and went downstairs to find Grant and another uniformed officer standing on his porch. "What's going on?"

"We had the silver tested, and we found Brian's fingerprints on it."

Hilliard shrugged. "So what?" He leaned against the doorframe. "You've seen the video, and that means that Brian didn't actually commit the burglary." He crossed his arms over his chest. "So I'll ask again, why are you here?"

"To make an arrest, of course," one of the officers said from behind Grant. Babycakes looked like he was barely old enough to shave.

Hilliard shook his head. "You can't. Brian was arrested and convicted of a burglary he didn't commit. He also did his time." He grinned as he glared at the officer. "Double jeopardy. You can't arrest and convict him for that same crime twice. That doesn't work." He turned back to Grant. "So why are you really here? I know you aren't that stupid." He left the implication hanging as he glanced at the other officer.

"But there's new evidence," the officer said. The guy looked like he should be wearing diapers rather than a uniform. Hilliard wanted to tell Babycakes to keep quiet, but he decided to instruct him instead.

"Of a crime that Brian has already been convicted of, and you can't try someone for the same crime twice." Hilliard was getting miffed with the rookie. "Grant, I suggest you talk now."

"We wanted to speak with Brian about what we found," he said.

Hilliard shrugged. "I'll see if he wants to speak with you." He debated about letting them inside and decided against it. "I'll be right back."

"I'm here," Brian said, wearing the same clothes he had last night as he stepped outside. "What is it you needed? I know no more than I did when I called you last night once I found the silver thing in my drawer. I didn't put it there, and like Hilliard said, it wouldn't matter if I did." He shifted his weight from foot to foot, clearly nervous. "I didn't commit that burglary in the first place."

"Yes, I know that," Grant said. "It's becoming clear that someone wanted to shift eyes back to you."

"You believe this guy?" Babycakes said.

"Yes, I do. I've seen the evidence, and he wasn't here when the burglary took place. He was out with his grandfather." Based on the look Grant gave him, Hilliard guessed that Babycakes would need a pacifier after the chewing-out he was going to get. "There's video proof, so put your own hasty conclusions aside and listen. You might learn something."

Babycakes snapped his mouth shut.

"Then what do you need?" Brian asked softly. Hilliard stood next to him and placed a hand gently at the base of his back. There was no way Hilliard was going to let Brian think he was in this alone. Besides, just the fact that Brian was going through this at all made him angry. He wanted to stand in front of him to protect him from everything the world had to throw his way.

"This seems very personal to me, and I'm trying to figure out who might have been able to do this," Grant said, and Hilliard rolled his eyes. "I know you think it's the original thief, but they would be much better off to simply keep their head down and wait for this whole thing to pass."

Hilliard cleared his throat. "Look, I think your logic is off. For most crimes, you would look in that direction, but not this one. Have you been able to confirm that this was one of the items stolen?" Grant nodded. "Good. Then there is hope that Violet will get more of her things back. But this also tells us that the thief is close to Violet. She's been ill and isn't going out of the house. That's what Beverly tells me. So someone close enough to her, who might visit when she's ill, could be the one we're after. We have a talk with her and explain what we have that will prove that Brian didn't commit the burglary, and suddenly something that had been stolen shows up in his drawer? Then Babycakes here is off on a tirade to arrest someone he can't. You're all looking the wrong way again, spinning your wheels, and the thief gets away with it once more." He was getting more than a little pissed off.

"Grant, everything I know I told you last night," Brian said gently. "I don't have any sudden insights, but I have to admit that I keep wondering who could hate me so much that they would do this to me." He sighed softly. "I never stole from anyone, and yet the police, the courts, all of them decided that I did, and I paid for that. My lawyer sucked, and I had no idea then. I did what he told me to do, and I spent time behind bars for a crime I didn't commit. So Hilliard and I are going to keep shaking the trees."

"You should leave police work to the professionals," Babycakes chimed in.

Brian scowled. "Right, because you're a real rocket scientist." Damn, Brian had a real set of claws. "I did that last time and look what happened." The tension between them was as thick as the fog outside.

"That's enough. Go sit on the car," Grant told Babycakes, and he stalked away.

"Where did they find him?" Brian snapped.

Grant rolled his eyes. "It's my job to train him and keep him out of trouble. I think he's going to be the reason I retire."

Hilliard shook his head. "Let me guess: Babycakes there is the sheriff's nephew?" He couldn't help smiling.

Grant hummed. "Sheriff's wife's nephew. I know it sounds like a bad sitcom, but in this case, life is stranger than fiction, and he's all mine." He turned to leave. "We'll keep on this."

"Thanks. So will we," Hilliard said. "We'll let you know if we find out anything concrete. Right now, I have a whole bunch of hunches but nothing to back any of them up."

Grant nodded. "Me too. Pick the most likely, test the waters, and see if it pans out. If not, move on to the next one. I've been doing this for a long time, and there are a couple of things I've learned. Sometimes hunches are right, but above all, follow the evidence… and the money. I've been trying to figure out who might have stood to gain from this theft, and that has left me stumped. No one seems to have come into extra cash, and the goods haven't hit the market as far as we can tell. Though I have to admit that with San Francisco and Los Angeles just hours way, goods come and go, disappearing into the city."

"True, and yet they end up in Brian's possession, which means that some of them are still around," Hilliard said. "Thank you for stopping by. If we find anything, we'll keep you informed." He saw him to the door.

Grant stepped out and began laughing. "Babycakes. I can't wait for that to get around the department." He continued laughing until Hilliard closed the door.

"That was weird." Hilliard was still trying to see the reason for the visit in the first place.

"Why? When it comes to this burglary and me, I've pretty much concluded that nothing is weird."

Hilliard sat down in the chair nearest the door. "No matter what happens, you can't be arrested or charged with a burglary that you've already been tried for. Grant knows that."

"Then why even come here with such a flimsy excuse?" Brian asked. "To harass me?" He sighed.

"Maybe to give the sheriff's nephew a lesson in keeping his mouth shut," Hilliard said. "Babycakes seems hotheaded, and obviously Grant knew there was nothing the police could do right now. But Babycakes had his undies in a twist, and now he's going back to the station with a new nickname he is going to spend years trying to live down." That was worth the morning visit alone. "What do you have to do today?"

"Thankfully, I'm busy. I have two stops to make for estimates. It seems that word really is getting around, and people are believing it."

Hilliard drew Brian close, wrapping his arms around his waist.

"Do you have any idea how much you've changed my life? I was trying to figure out how I was going to make anything happen. Now things are really turning around."

"That's good. But we need to put this entire issue to bed, though that is going to have to wait a few days. I need to get some of my own work done so I can pass this exam and gain admittance to the bar." Hilliard felt a yawn trying to emerge and did his best to stifle it, resting his head against Brian's flat belly instead. "I know you should head home so you can change and get ready for work. I need to shower and then get my books so I can prepare. But how about we meet this weekend and maybe we can pay a few visits? There are people we need to talk to and take the measure of."

"Do you think Violet might help us?" Brian asked. "We're going to need it if we're to talk to the people I'm thinking of."

"We can try. But I have a few ideas of my own." He closed his eyes, loving the feel of Brian against him. "We'll have to think on it a little." He sighed. "Will you come back after work?"

"Once I check on Gran and make sure she has dinner and stuff…." Brian seemed happy, and Hilliard found he was the same. But he had no illusions that there weren't going to be plenty of bumps in the road still to come.

Chapter 12

"ARE YOU sure you're okay? I know I've been gone quite a bit, and I don't want you to think I'm abandoning you."

"I'm fine. I have my shows to watch. Besides, I'm happy you're seeing someone and getting out of the house. You need a life of your own."

"I know. But I don't want you to spend all your time sitting in your chair with nothing to do."

She waved at him. "I'm fine. The night is clear, and it's going to be pretty. I may sit outside and look at the stars. I don't get to do that very often. The dogs will be here after you walk them, and if there's anything I need, I always have the telephone. Now go on and have yourself a nice evening." Gran turned back to the television, but Brian stayed where he was. "Is something wrong?"

"I don't know. Hill says that he's going to take the state bar exam so he can practice here, but he still hasn't said if he's staying." He sat down across from her. "Am I being really dumb? He could be leaving in a little while. It isn't like he has anything to keep him here, and he could practice law back home. I'm starting to wonder if I've already let myself get in too deep and I'm going to end up shattered if he doesn't decide to stay."

Gran set down her cup on the table next to her. "But what if he does? You like him, and you two get along. What if he passes the exam and decides to open a practice out of the house? He could do that. The town could use a lawyer here. Usually we have to go to Ukiah or Fort Bragg for anything like that."

"I know. But…." He was suddenly so unsure. "I mean… am I being stupid for not being more careful?"

Gran chuckled softly. "Do you know what happens to men who are careful when it comes to love? We have a word for them: bachelors. They may meet the right person, but by the time they decide and make their move, it's too late. I don't want you to be too late." She leaned forward. "I can also tell you that hearts heal and people move on. The ones filled with regret are those who didn't take the chance at all." She patted his hand. "Go on and have yourself a fun night. Don't worry about the doubt and stuff. Just let yourself be happy. You deserve it." She smiled and released his hand. Brian thanked her and left the house, taking the dogs with him, walking down the street and over toward Hilliard's.

THE DOGS pulled harder as he got closer, their excitement growing. They knew Hilliard was a soft touch for treats. Brian knocked on the door. All the lights were on, so he opened it and peered inside, calling.

"Hilliard?"

"Come on in," he called.

"I hope it's okay. I needed to take the dogs for a walk. They haven't been out of the house much and—" He continued through the living room but stopped when he saw a strange man with an arm thrown over Hilliard's shoulder. "I'm sorry…." He had no idea who this guy was. Maybe he should just leave.

"Of course the dogs are welcome." Hilliard moved away and knelt down. Poppy and Gigi hurried over to get their pets and of course a bit of dog treat. "Hey, girls, are you being good for Beverly?" he crooned gently, and they swarmed over each other to give him kisses, generally in doggie heaven. Eventually Hilliard straightened up. "Brian, this is Al. He and I went to college together. Not to be confused with Alan. This guy isn't a *complete* asshole."

"Gee, thanks." Al smirked.

"How long are you staying?" Hilliard hadn't mentioned anything about having guests.

"I had a meeting in San Francisco with clients for a few days, and they got done early. So I figured I'd look up Hill here and see what he was up to. I had no idea the place you inherited was hours away from civilization. My God, it took forever to get here. There were times when I figured the guys from *Deliverance* were going to jump out of the trees at any moment." He grinned as though he had made a joke. Brian didn't get it. "I got a room at the Hill House for the night, and I'll drive back to the city tomorrow."

"Seems like a long way to say hello," Brian said softly. He didn't know why he was so suspicious. Maybe it was the way Al watched him with big dark eyes. The guy reminded Brian of a shark.

"Not really. I heard Hill inherited this house and figured that by now he had to be going stir-crazy." He sipped from a glass of white wine. Brian was starting to wonder if he should go, except he didn't trust this guy for a second and didn't want Hilliard alone with him. This was a smooth talker who was used to getting whatever he wanted. Brian had met people like him in jail—guys who seemed all smiley, but behind your back, they would steal anything they could get their hands on.

"Like you said, it's a long way to go." Brian accepted a beer and thanked Hilliard. The dogs patrolled the kitchen, probably to see if there were any wayward snacks, before heading to the living room.

"You make it sound like I'm in the middle of nowhere," Hilliard said. "Did you get a look at the view as you drove up? It's gorgeous here, and though it's a ways from the city, this town has everything I need." Hilliard met Brian's gaze with a slight wink. "Go on into the living room and I'll be right in."

Brian went in to find the dogs on the sofa, watching him. He sat down, and Gigi lay down to his right with Poppy on his left. They watched Al but made no effort to get his attention.

"How long have you lived here?" Al asked.

"Most of my life. I have my own business and help care for my grandmother," Brian answered. "What do you do?"

"I'm a lawyer like Hill. He and I did prelaw together. We went to different law schools but took the bar at the same time." Al looked toward the kitchen and called out, "I'm still trying to figure out how you got a better score than me." The guy was teasing, but there was an edge in his voice, like he thought he should always be at the top of everything. "Hill clerked after law school, and then he and Alan opened their own practice. I joined a firm, and now I'm a partner."

"Carter and Garrett," Hilliard said as he came into the room with a plate of cheese and crackers that he set on the coffee table.

"Yeah. I'm doing a lot of work at the federal level now." Like that meant anything to Brian, but it sounded impressive. "I heard about you and Alan." He set his glass on the coffee table. "You know, when you come back to Cleveland, you should stop by and see me. I already talked to the other partners at my firm, and they would be interested in making a place for you. They all know your work, and a number of them have stood against you in court. They were more than a little impressed."

Hilliard sat down. "They were good and well prepared."

"But you still beat us more times than not," Al said. "You won cases that you shouldn't have a few times. Got the judges to see things in a slightly new way." He sat back, one leg crossed over another as though he owned the world. "That got the attention of the rest of the firm."

Brian felt the room go cold. This guy was here to offer Hilliard a job—and a good one, if Brian understood right. He should have known something like this would happen.

"I'm flattered, and I appreciate the offer…."

"This is what you've always wanted, remember? We both wanted the partnership in a big firm. You have clients who will come over just as soon as you return to the city. You'd be an asset. We all know it."

Hilliard didn't say yes, but he didn't say no either, and there was a slight smile on his lips, and he leaned forward as though he wanted to hear more. It was the curiosity that caught Brian's breath in his throat. He had always known somewhere deep down that Hilliard would be called back to his own life. There wasn't all that much here for him, if Brian was honest. This was a small town tucked away on the rugged north coast of California, hours away from the things Hilliard would have come to expect. There were limited opportunities here, and now one had just come knocking from the outside. Brian couldn't blame Hilliard for being interested.

"I do appreciate the offer," Hilliard said with a smile.

"Then when I get back, I'll talk to the others, arrange to fly you back so you can meet everyone, sit down, and talk some business. I think it would be a great change for us to work together, and you'll like the firm. It's everything we always wanted." Al smiled again, and Brian stood.

"I think I should be going. There's no need for me to interrupt your time together." The truth was, he needed to get the hell out of here, and he couldn't do it fast enough. Brian called the dogs toward the door and put their leashes on.

"Brian, I—" Hilliard began, but Brian cut him off.

"You have a good visit," Brian told Al. "And I'll see you." He opened the door and stepped out into the night before striding home as quickly as he could.

BRIAN HAD jobs lined up all day, and his clients didn't need to see that he was more tired than before he went to bed. He drank his second cup of coffee and filled a large thermos with the rest of the pot before leaving the house and heading to his first job before he got interrogated about what happened… again. Gran was still in her bedroom, though he had heard her get up. He called to her from the door, and she told him to have a good day. Then he climbed into his truck and headed off toward his job in Little River, a few miles down the coast.

It was funny how a simple job could turn into more. He did all he could for Martin before he left, then made a list of additional items to complete on a return visit. After shaking Martin's hand, he packed up and called his next client to let them know he was on his way.

As he approached the turn off the main road, his phone dinged with a message. He continued down the winding private drive, watching the numbers, before turning off and going up a steep incline to a home situated on the only bit of level ground. He climbed out and checked the message from Hilliard.

Do you want to meet for dinner? I have something to talk to you about. It was followed by a smiley face. Brian sighed and sent a thumbs-up before shoving his phone in his pocket and going to meet his client. This job also took longer than expected. Brian was glad he didn't have spare time, because when he gave himself a moment, all he did was think about Hilliard and the fact that he was leaving.

By the time he finished his final stop of the day, twilight shone over the water. He made his way back toward Mendocino. It had been a long day, but profitable. He stopped just off the main road and messaged Hilliard that he was getting to town and going to clean up before coming over. Then he headed to Gran's.

"Who kicked your dog?" Gran asked.

"What?"

"Why the long face? What happened—did someone cancel or give you a hard time?" Gran sounded about ready to kill.

"My jobs went fine." Brian went right to the kitchen to grab a bottle of cold water, which he downed in a few gulps before tossing the empty into recycling.

"So it's something else. Hilliard?" Gran asked.

"Just stay out of it."

Gran smiled, following him with her eyes as he returned to the room. "So it is him. What happened?"

"A friend of his is in town to offer him a big job at his firm… back in Cleveland." He made a face and wished he had just gone upstairs, because Gran was not going to let this go.

"Did he say he was taking the job?" Gran asked.

Brian shook his head. "But you should have seen his face, Gran. It was like Al was offering him everything he ever wanted, and all I could do was sit there. I felt like a fool. There's nothing I can offer him here. It's a small town, and…." He huffed. "I knew this would happen."

Gran rolled her eyes. "Is Hilliard gone?"

"No."

"Has he said he's leaving?" Gran asked, and Brian shook his head. "Then you don't know squat. So some guy came in here with a job offer. If you ask me, you need to give Hilliard a reason to stay and not come back here with your tail between your legs. If you want Hilliard, then win him. That's what Chester did for me."

"How?"

Gran wrinkled her nose. "First thing, go upstairs, shower, and get cleaned up, because you stink. Then put on something nice and maybe a little sexy. Then go over there and give him a reason to stay." She winked.

"He said he had something to tell me." Brian just knew it was something he didn't want to hear and was trying to put it off.

"Then go clean up and find out what it is. You're just assuming that you know and catastrophizing. Stop it. Go over and see what he has to say." She shook her head. "It may be something good. Now go before my nose decides to run for the hills, because you stink." She waved him away, and Brian trudged upstairs and went right to the bathroom.

Gran was right: he stank. As soon as he stripped off and got under the water, he started to feel better. At least he was clean and could get his heart broken without smelling like a swamp.

"TAKE THE dogs with you," Gran said as Brian got ready to leave. She was still sitting in her chair, and Brian wondered if she was in pain. Sometimes she barely got out of the chair, and he was getting worried that if she didn't get up and move around more often, she wouldn't be able to at all. "And stop in the garden to cut some flowers to take with you."

"Gran," Brian said, rolling his eyes. "That's so… predictable."

"Then do things your way," she said. "But take the dogs. They need to go out, and a walk will do them good." She slowly got out of her chair and headed toward the kitchen.

"I can make you something to eat before I go."

"I'm fine. You go and have some fun. I'll have a light dinner." She waved him off, and Brian got the leashes, admonishing the dogs that tangling them around his legs was not nice, especially when Poppy decided to immediately try running in circles around him.

"Stop," he said sharply. Poppy sat, looking up at him with her big eyes, probably wondering why he had paused her fun. She blinked while he untangled the lead and then got Gigi's on. "Bye, Gran."

"Have fun, sweetheart," she called back, and he stepped out into the cool, slightly damp evening air.

"Come on. Let's go see Hilliard and find out what he wants." He led them down the street, the dogs half prancing with excitement. As soon as they caught sight of the house, both dogs began pulling, trying to tug him closer. As Brian approached the front door, Hilliard opened it, and Brian let the dogs run right up to Hilliard, who lavished them both with attention.

He waited for Brian and ushered them all inside, then took off the leads and let the dogs roam the house. "I guess they're excited."

"They were in the house most of the day and needed some exercise." Brian smiled as Hilliard swept him into a hug and then kissed him. Within a fraction of a second, all his concerns flew from his mind as Hilliard held him tightly, deepening the kiss until he couldn't think straight.

Brian held still, holding Hilliard in return, hoping like hell that his knees didn't give out. "What was that for?" he asked when Hilliard backed away a few seconds later. "I mean…."

"I missed you, and…." Hilliard's breath came in pants, and Brian smiled. He loved the way Hilliard's eyes glassed over and the way he tilted first to one side and then the other like he was off-balance and his head spun as much as Brian's did.

"Okay. I like that you did." He rested his head on Hilliard's shoulder. Then he straightened up. "How did the visit go with your friend?" Brian needed to know what was happening there, and he was already bracing for bad news.

"Okay. We talked, and then he went back to his inn for the night. He and I had breakfast this morning, and then he headed back to the city."

Brian nodded. "I wasn't sure how long he was going to stay." He might have said, but Brian's mind had been on other things, like Hilliard's job offer and him moving away. "Do you have calls and stuff scheduled?"

"What for?"

"His job offer?" Brian felt confused.

"God, I would never work with Al. He would drive me crazy. Way too competitive, and not in a good way. Every case that he won would be compared to the cases I won. It would be a dick-measuring contest for the rest of my life." Hilliard grinned. "And we both know that mine is bigger." Brian snickered, because that was something he couldn't argue with. "Besides, yeah, I think I'd have loved working at a large law firm with their resources, but I got too used to being my own boss. I liked calling the shots and deciding if I wanted to take on a client or not. I did pro bono work because I believed in the client, but all that would be up to the managing partner instead of me." He sighed. "Big firms have their advantages, but in the end it's all about the bottom line."

"So you aren't leaving?" Brian asked, finally allowing himself the chance to voice his real concern.

"Not to work with Al. He's a good friend, but nothing more than that, and I'm not going to take a job with his firm. Yeah, I bet they'd like to have me, and that feels pretty good, but I'm still trying to figure out what would make me happy." Hilliard held Brian's shoulders in his big hands. "If I'm honest, being here with you makes me happy, but if I stay here, I'm going to spend the rest of my life writing wills and doing property deeds. I loved being in the thick of things, arguing cases, because that's what I'm really good at." He looked around the room.

"Then you need to go where you can get what you need," Brian said, darkness closing in around his mood.

"That's just it—I don't know if there is a place like that, so I'm trying to figure out what I want to do. I know I need to make a decision soon…." He sighed and pulled away, walking toward the kitchen. "This probably sounds really stupid, but so far things have just happened as far as my career. It was Alan's idea to open the firm, and he was the real force behind it. I wanted to build a firm, and together I thought we would both get what we wanted. It didn't work out that way." He stopped. "I love it here, and I love the people here." Hilliard kept his gaze glued on Brian to the point that he tugged at his collar. "I just want to make sure that I make the right decision."

Brian could understand that. "So is this… whatever is between us just filler until you figure out what you want?" It always seemed like his life was on hold because of what someone else wanted or did.

"No," Hilliard said firmly and closed the gap between them. "That is not what's happening. I would never do that to anyone. I just need a chance to get my crap together. Okay?" Damn the man and his puppy-dog eyes. "Anyway, I have some good news. There's a festival this weekend, and I have it on good authority—mainly from Ruth—that Violet's son Frank is going to be staffing one of the booths for the local baseball league, and I thought that we might be able to get a few minutes to talk to him. I also think that if he's there, then it's likely his kids will be as well, and maybe we can talk to them and their friends."

"How are we going to do that? They aren't going to want to have anything to do with me."

"No, they probably aren't. But once we talk to Frank, maybe we can talk to the other parents. They'll all be there."

"And they'll be busy," Brian countered.

"True. But word has definitely gotten around, and I have a few tricks up my sleeve." He grinned. "Besides, I have a way of getting people to open up. Remember Violet? Just leave it to me."

"Do you even want me there?" Brian asked. "Maybe they'll talk to you if I'm not around."

Hilliard shook his head. "I want them to look you in the eye and tell their stories. Someone here robbed Violet and pinned it on you. I want to see who flinches first."

"Okay," Brian said. "Are we going to have dinner?"

Hilliard pulled him until they were chest to chest. "I was thinking we could start with dessert." He kissed Brian hard, making the earth move under his feet, before backing away and leading Brian toward the stairs.

Chapter 13

"Jesus," Brian whispered as Hilliard tugged off the last of his clothes. Damn, Hilliard loved the way this man looked, with his corded, lean muscle that left him drooling. That was okay, because Hilliard wanted to lick him all over. "What you do to me."

"I haven't done anything yet," Hilliard whispered back, kicking the door closed as he heard the dogs coming up the stairs. He loved those two, but he adored Brian more. And damn it all, his entire body shook with delicious anticipation.

Brian swallowed hard, his legs quivering as Hilliard climbed on the bed, straddling him as he stalked his way up his body. "You make me want things I never thought I could have again." He licked a circle around Brian's pebbled nipple, receiving a groan and a shiver.

"Why do you think that?" Brian asked.

Hilliard grew quiet. The last thing he wanted to talk about at this moment was Alan and all the shit he'd put Hilliard through. They both deserved better than that, and he'd be damned if he was going to let his ex intrude on a moment of passion. Instead, he sucked the other nipple, loving the shiver, before kissing Brian with everything he had. "I want you," he whispered.

"You have me," Brian said in return, drawing Hilliard down against him, their heat melding until it threatened to scorch the sheets. "Any way you want me."

"Oh yeah." Hilliard loved the way Brian's lips parted and his eyes sparkled. He wanted him to look like that all the time. He'd seen his eyes filled with worry so many times in the weeks they had known each other. "Then I'll take what I want." He cocked an eyebrow before slinking down Brian's body, then sucked his cock between his lips, taking him as far as he could.

"Jesus!" Brian cried as Hilliard bobbed his head, determined to drive Brian out of his mind. He tasted good—salty, a touch of bitterness, but all man, and damn, Hilliard wanted as much of that as he could get. Brian's breathing became shallow, and he clamped his eyes closed.

Hilliard backed away and brought their lips together, letting Brian taste a little of himself on his tongue. "I want you now."

Brian nodded, and Hilliard nearly dumped the nightstand on its side, but he found a condom and rolled it on with a shaking hand. He also found the slick and used it liberally before sliding a finger inside Brian's smoldering body.

There were things that Hilliard knew he would never forget, and the first time with Brian was one of them. The man was more than hot; he was like a live wire, surrounding him, tugging him deep, taking Hilliard to the moon. It was like no other sensation he had ever experienced. At first Hilliard didn't dare move, but then he rocked slowly, and Brian moved with him.

He leaned over him, sliding in and out of Brian's body, loving every single second. Whenever he pulled away, Brian drew him back in. Hilliard needed him like an addict needed a fix, and he knew he was never going to be the same. No one compared to this. He thought he and Alan had fit together, but he knew now that they hadn't, not really. Being with Brian was perfection, physically and emotionally. He had told himself that if things didn't work out, he could always return to Cleveland, but he knew now that no matter what, he had to make sure this relationship that he had with Brian worked out. He could barely breathe, and yet he wanted more. Brian urged him to move, and Hilliard went right along with it, letting Brian guide him to a place of sheer bliss.

"Hilly… don't stop," Brian whimpered, stroking himself as he wound his legs around Hilliard's back.

"Won't." It was all he could manage.

"Don't you dare," Brian growled. "Now fuck me into next week. I want to feel you when I'm working tomorrow." He pushed against Hilliard, burying his cock to the hilt.

Hilliard leaned closer, kissing Brian hard. "You like the dirty talk?"

"Hell yes," Brian groaned. "Give me your cock. I want it all." He clamped down, and Hilliard gasped from the pleasure. This was a side of Brian he hadn't expected, and it was sexy as hell. Brian put his hands over his head, stretching that incredible body, his eyes wide, his mouth open. He was gorgeous, to say the least, and the way he lay, it was like he was giving himself to Hilliard. That kind of trust spurred him forward faster, harder, Brian swaying under him as the bed rocked back and forth with their movement.

"And I want you. Every bit of you." He thrust deeply, gasping right along with Brian. Sweat broke out on both of them, Brian glistening in the light coming through the window, his scent, musky and rich, filling the room. Hilliard snapped his hips and then rolled them, watching Brian, listening to his breathing. "That's it. Tell me what you like." He tweaked his nipples once, then harder. Brian gasped as Hilliard thrust again, throwing his head back as the sensation threatened to overwhelm him.

"Then take it." He pulled Hilliard down, grabbing his ass and using his hands to press Hilliard to him.

Hilliard stopped. "You don't get to top from the bottom, sweetheart." He moved only slowly, earning a growl from Brian, whose eyes glazed over. It was clear he wanted more and that Hilliard was driving him crazy, but that was his intention. He brushed Brian's hand away from his cock and replaced it with his, stroking him slowly.

"Jesus, you're killing me."

"Then you need to take what I give you." He had never been much for dirty talk in the past, but with Brian, it was a real mind fuck. Brian was as vocal as a first-rate porn star, and that was sexy as all hell.

Brian kept up his vocal barrage, swearing a blue streak under his breath until Hilliard sped up, driving into Brian as he stroked his beefy cock harder and faster. The groans and *fucks* came louder, and it was clear that Brian was as on the edge as Hilliard, but he wasn't ready to bring this to an end, so he slowed down once more, giving them both a chance to breathe, before giving in to Brian.

The bed rocked more quickly, and Hilliard hoped the damned thing didn't collapse as he and Brian barreled closer. His skin tingled and his cock throbbed as he tried to hold off for a little longer.

"Gonna come," Brian ground out between his teeth. "So close…."

Hilliard slowed his movements, holding them both right on the edge for as long as he dared before letting them both tumble into sweet, mind-blowing release that left Hilliard breathless and unable to think for a long time.

When he could move, Hilliard disposed of the condom and quickly cleaned up the mess he'd made beside the bed. He climbed into bed, and Brian came in from the bathroom and lay down next to him. "Are you sure about all this?" Brian asked.

"About what?" He held Brian to him and closed his eyes. "Whatever you're worried about, just relax and don't think about it now."

"But…," Brian probed.

Hilliard sighed. "I can almost guarantee you're overthinking. I like it here. What I need to do is figure out how to make it work. And as for our thief in hiding… they can't stay that way forever. There's information out there, and we will find it. I promise you that." He lightly kissed the top of Brian's head.

Brian tilted his head upward. "What if we stir up something that puts us both in danger?"

Hilliard sighed. "As much as I want to say full steam ahead, I've been thinking the same thing." He smiled. "They broke into your grandmother's house to try to plant evidence. What will they do if they're cornered?" He'd been wondering that for days. "They broke into your truck before." Brian met his gaze. "But then I keep thinking that if we don't put a stop to this, they're going to hurt other people. The initial robbery might have been two years ago, but they are escalating to keep trying to cover it up."

"True. But what if they hurt you?" Brian asked, and Hilliard held him tighter. "I don't want anything to happen to you."

Hilliard closed his eyes and lay back on the pillow. "You know, this has to be the strangest pillow talk in history. People usually say sweet things to each other. You and I, we try to find a thief." He smiled. "Do you think that's some sort of kink?"

Brian chuckled. "Somehow I doubt it qualifies until we shout evidence at each other or try to identify possible clues while we're having sex." He devolved into laughter. "Or shout, 'Colonel Mustard did it in the ballroom with the rope' to make you come."

"God," Hilliard gasped as he joined in the mirth. "You're something else." It had been a long time since he'd met anyone like Brian, and the more time he spent with him, the more his heart told him exactly what it wanted. The problem was that his head was way too damned practical, and he needed to make sure that he wasn't going to end up right back where he'd been a few months ago, on the outside looking into his own life, trying to pick up the pieces. Brian wasn't Alan, he knew that, but maybe he was just a little gun-shy.

"I like to think so." Brian lifted his head once more, meeting Hilliard's gaze. "I have to ask you something. You inherited this house…

and Alan was a real asshole…. You're out of the business, and he's paid you off. So if I wasn't in the picture here, what would you be doing right now?" He hoisted his eyebrows.

Hilliard rolled his eyes. "Probably studying for the bar exam so I could get my license here and looking to either join a firm or start one of my own. I have the cash, and with the house, I could remodel the garage storage building into an office and hang out a shingle."

"Then why not do that?" Brian asked. "Take me out of the equation and stop worrying about what will happen between us. I'm not Alan, and I'm not going to hurt you the way he did. I would never cheat on anyone. But forget about all that."

"I can't. What if things don't work out? You live three blocks away. This is a tiny town where everyone knows everyone else and the gossip mill is fueled by tea and runs overtime. We would never get a chance to be away from each other."

Brian rolled his eyes. "Look, regardless of what happens, we decide that we'll be friends. If things don't work out and we go our separate ways, we have to agree that we will always be friends and… maybe with benefits, because those are some benefits, let me tell you." He grinned slyly, and Hilliard snorted instead of laughing. "All I'm saying is don't make your decisions based on what's happened before. I'm not a jerk and neither are you. So we can do this…." He leaned closer. "Unless."

Hilliard swallowed. "What?"

"Unless this has nothing to do with that at all. Did Al get you thinking?" Brian drew closer, and Hilliard looked away. "He did. That old dream of yours that you were so close to, he brought it back. And now the vision of a small practice here in California doesn't quite seem to measure up."

Hilliard shook his head, even though he knew there was some truth to what Brian had said. "I don't know. That's the sucky part. While I could never work with Al…."

"He made you want what he has," Brian filled in, and Hilliard nodded. There was no use denying the truth.

"That's what I'm trying to figure out. This is a crossroads for me, and if I take you out of the equation, then that's what I'm left with. But you *are* in the equation. You're here in my arms right now, and I like that so much. I look forward to when you come over or when I come down to visit. My heart jumps a little when you send me a message, and I like that. So I go back and forth." He kissed Brian gently. "But I always seem to end up on the side of wanting to stay. I really do like it here." He just wished he could figure out what it was that kept him from chucking it in and committing to a new life.

HILLIARD WALKED toward the house as Brian came out with Beverly holding his arm. "Are you sure you want to go?" Brian asked her softly.

Beverly smacked him on the shoulder. "I'm not dead yet," she admonished and continued down the walk. The dogs hurried after her and climbed into the back seat of Hilliard's Mustang as soon as he opened the door. They had their feet on the folded top, looking out like they were the queens of the world as Brian got Beverly settled in the front seat. He climbed in back and got as comfortable as possible.

"I'm glad we don't have to go very far. Otherwise I'd never be able to unfold my legs." He pulled the seat back, and Hilliard got in, helped Beverly make a little more room for Brian, and then they were off.

"Do they do this every year?"

"Yes. They didn't during COVID, but that's about it." Beverly seemed happy, and Hilliard liked when Brian settled his hand on his shoulder. "It's all for the benefit of the Civic Club. They put this on every year and use the proceeds to help improve the village."

"I remember going to this when I was a kid. They used to have carnival games, and I remember the year that I won all that candy." Brian chuckled. "Gran took it and only let me have it a little at a time."

"Can you blame me? You won at least half a dozen packages of chocolate. It was self-preservation, if you ask me. If you had eaten all that chocolate at one time, I'd have had to peel you off the ceiling." Beverly seemed so happy. When they approached the carnival, Hilliard showed Beverly's placard for special parking, and the volunteers directed him to a place near the entrance.

The afternoon sun was making an appearance, so Hilliard left the top down, got Poppy on her leash, and took charge of her. Once Beverly was out of the car, Brian wrangled Gigi.

"What's the game plan?" Beverly asked.

"You have a good time and leave the questions to Hilliard," Brian said.

"Poppycock. I want to shake down a suspect and make him crack," Beverly teased. "I'd love it if I could get Frank in the hot seat. I'd like to see that weasel squirm."

"Gran…."

She huffed. "Don't worry. I'll be good." She patted Brian on the shoulder. Hilliard had a pretty good idea that if she got the chance, she had every intention of ignoring that promise.

"What do you want to do first?" Brian asked.

"Business before pleasure. I'll go find Frank and see if we can shake a few leaves off the trees while you and Beverly see if you can find his kids."

"What do we do if we find them?" Brian asked.

Hilliard smiled. "Scare them a little—and I know just how to do it." He told Brian and Beverly exactly what he had in mind.

THE BASEBALL team booth wasn't quite what Hilliard expected. He thought it would be hot dogs and popcorn, but they were selling raffle tickets and something called sour-cream-and-chive fries. The older boys seemed to know the routine and made up the orders while the others helped customers, and a man nearing fifty oversaw everything. "Can I help you?" he asked Hilliard when he saw him watching.

"It's like a well-oiled machine." Hilliard smiled.

"We've been doing this for a while now." He joined Hilliard out front. "I have one of the fathers in back cooking the fries, and the boys take it from there. These are an absolute favorite here." He looked Hilliard over. "Are you a tourist or new in town?"

"I used to come here when I was a kid. I'm Grace Bauman's great-nephew. She left me the house in her will, and I'm fixing it up and trying to figure out if I should resettle here. It's a real nice place."

"Frank Trainer. And it really is." He shook Hilliard's hand. "This is a special sort of place. It's got a unique history of its own, and whenever you live here, you get immersed in the way this location gets wrapped up in your soul. Once Mendo gets inside, you never really want to leave." He took a minute to help one of the boys before returning.

"How is the crime here? I've heard some rumors about a few burglaries." Hilliard tilted his head slightly. "Trainer… why is that familiar? Yeah, Ruth was telling me that family was robbed some time ago."

Frank's expression didn't change much, but the redness around his neck slipped upward. "That was my mother, and they caught the guy." He sounded confident.

"That's great. Was it recently? Ruth told me that the person they caught didn't really do it." He leaned closer. "One thing I found out—she loves to talk. I sat next to her at a church function, and she regaled me with stories." Maybe he was laying it on thick, but he needed so see Frank's reaction. "According to her, apparently the man they caught was somewhere else with his grandfather. I really hope they find the real thief. It must be nerve-racking to have that sort of thing happen in a place like this." He sighed. "I'm very sorry for you and your family's loss. I hope they find the real thief soon." He stepped away to place an order for some fries and a raffle ticket before leaving the booth.

He turned like he was going to leave, but instead he settled on a bench under a nearby tree to eat and watch. Frank spoke to a man and his son as they approached the booth, and then Frank was off, striding around the edge of the field like a man on a mission.

Keeping him in sight, Hilliard tossed the empty package into a nearby trash can and followed Frank toward town. There were plenty of people around him as cover. Frank didn't seem too concerned about being seen or followed, though Hilliard did his best to stay out of sight. As he rounded the corner toward the main street, he paused as Frank stood outside the grocery store and pulled out his phone.

"Where are you?" he asked. "I need to talk to you now." He waited. "I'm near the pub." He hung up, and Hilliard stayed across the street and watched through the crowds of people as Frank began pacing. Pretty soon, his two sons hurried up, both looking pale and worried.

"What did you tell Grandma?" one of the boys demanded as soon as they saw their father. "She sent people to talk to Kevin and me. I think she thinks we were the ones who stole her stuff." He seemed truly upset, and Hilliard drew closer so he could hear better.

"Apparently the guy who was convicted has been proven innocent, and now your grandmother is determined to find out who really stole from her." The look he gave his boys told Hilliard plenty. Frank thought one or both of the boys could be the culprits.

"But we didn't do it," Kendall said. "We'd never steal from Gran." They each looked at the other, their expressions totally confused. Hilliard lost sight of them for a few seconds as a group of people passed in front of them, talking loudly.

"So help me, if either of you…." He glared at the boys, and Hilliard tried to put together what he was seeing.

"We never did. You should know that." They seemed affronted and surprised at their father's questioning.

"Like many people would believe you," Frank said with a glare. Jesus, these boys had a tough road ahead of them if their father didn't trust them. Granted, from what Hilliard had seen and gathered from others, these kids weren't known for their good behavior, but he could only imagine how much it hurt to have your parent doubt you like that.

"But it wasn't us," they said in unison, loudly enough for Hilliard to hear clearly. He turned away and headed back toward the carnival, mulling over the information. It was possible the boys were lying, but they truly seemed upset and affronted. Unless they were great actors, he doubted it was them, which was a disappointment. It made sense for them to be the thieves. They might have known where the valuables were kept. And Frank… would he steal from his mother? Hilliard doubted it, especially with the way he went to find the boys. It seemed to Hilliard that Frank had thought it might have been them, and he wouldn't have done that if he were guilty.

Hilliard used the crowd as cover, heading along with the flow of people back toward the carnival. He found Brian and his grandmother sitting on a bench near the entrance to the area. "Did you find out anything?" Brian asked.

"I think I did." He sat down. "After I casually mentioned the alleged thief's innocence, Frank called the boys right away, and they met up, but I don't think any of them did it. Frank was afraid the boys had done it. And I think the boys were afraid their father had done it. They turned nearly completely white when he asked them about it."

"No one in that family talks to one another," Beverly said. "Frank is one of those fathers who yells and makes demands, so everyone either stays away from him as best they can, or they say yes and then do what they want when his back is turned."

Hilliard leaned forward so he could see both of them. "Can you imagine thinking that someone else in your family committed a burglary, then covered it up, and not talking about it? You continue like that for years and just let it go."

Brian shrugged. "Why not? They had the thief in jail and they could all just carry on. It wasn't like they had to give it a thought anymore. I was paying the price for it, and they went on with their miserable, useless lives." The anger in Brian's eyes was strong and deep.

"Maybe we should go," Hilliard offered. "I should have given more thought to how all of this would make you feel." Dammit. To him this was about unraveling a mystery and solving a puzzle. Yes, he cared about Brian and wanted him to be vindicated, but he was still a step removed from what had happened. That wasn't the case for Brian. This was his life, and he had lived with being accused of something he hadn't done for years now.

"No," he snapped. "I'm fine." He sighed through his nose, his eyes softening a little, but the anger was still there, and Hilliard resolved to see this all the way through.

Beverly took Brian's arm and leaned closer to him. "Remember that in order to help, you need to keep your mind clear and think. This isn't going to be solved by emotion and old hurt, but by reason and figuring out the facts." She got Brian to look away from Frank, who had taken up his place at the baseball team booth once more.

"Okay, so what do we know?" Brian asked, glancing over at Frank once more before turning his attention to Hilliard.

"First, we know that whoever did this knew Violet would be out of the house. They had to know the window of opportunity. Also, it had to be someone who was close enough to Violet to know where she kept her valuables, because the room wasn't ransacked. The thieves took small items of value and knew where they were. That led me to think it was the boys or Frank, but I'm not so sure anymore." Hilliard lowered his gaze.

Beverly cleared her throat. "We know that whoever it was broke into Brian's truck and the house to plant evidence."

Hilliard nodded. "And on that note, they knew that Brian had been out of town and that his grandfather had passed away." He paused a few minutes to think. "I know this is a small town, but that's a lot of details to know in order to be able to pull all this off."

Brian nodded too. "I agree, and it doesn't seem like kids to me. I mean sure, maybe Violet's grandkids knew where she kept stuff, but I don't see the boys as being plugged deeply into the town gossip mill." He sighed once more, his shoulders slumping. "Maybe we'll never be able to figure this out. It's been a long time since it happened."

"True, but not for the thief. After all, as soon as they got word that we might be able to prove your innocence, they planted more evidence to lead everyone back to you." There were still so many things Hilliard didn't understand, but the picture was coming into focus. He just needed a few more pieces. "Sometimes I wish I were Sherlock Holmes or something."

Beverly laughed. "Please. He had to figure out the mystery before the end of the book, and almost every time, there were obscure facts that most people don't know involved in solving the mystery. This is real life, and as much as we'd all like to have things ordered and wrapped up in a neat bow, it doesn't always happen. But I agree—we are still missing information. I'm just not sure where to get it."

Brian sat back on the bench, and Hilliard did the same. "Maybe we need to talk to Violet again. She wants answers as much as we do," Brian offered.

"That's not a bad idea," Beverly said. "There are some questions I'd like to ask her myself, grandmother to grandmother." She leaned forward slightly and got herself to her feet. "Let's go have some fun for a while. We've done what we can for tonight."

Hilliard knew she was right. Brian nodded and pointed. "There's that game I used to play, with all the candy."

Beverly shook her head. "You don't need candy, and you can buy all you want yourself."

"True, but what if I really want to win one of those giant stuffed pandas?" Brian countered.

"We don't need any of that stuff," Beverly said with a smile. "You two go on and have fun. I see Ruth over by the popcorn booth. I'm going to say hello." She shooed them off. "Go on." She smiled, and Brian didn't waste any time, leading Hilliard toward the games area. He seemed like a kid again. Hilliard laughed and went right along with him.

"What do you want to play?" Brian asked.

Hilliard grinned. "How about the target game over there?"

Brian scoffed. "That's so rigged."

"Really?" Hilliard asked with a wink as he headed over to the booth where some luckless kids were shooting cork guns at paper cup targets.

"You get three shots for two bucks," the guy in the booth said with a smile. Hilliard handed over two bills and looked at the gun. He watched the kids, sighted the gun, and then shot and hit the first cup. He took his second shot and then the third, hitting all three times. Then he turned to the operator of the booth, shaking his head before asking the kids for the guns. He took a look and then handed them back.

"All the sights are off. They were probably made that way, so the guns shoot low. So raise them up and aim high." He smiled as the kids began knocking the cups off the top shelf, where the operator had placed the higher-value prize cups, figuring no one would hit them. Hilliard collected his Nintendo Switch top prize, and so did the kids. "I suggest you close your booth and clean up this game. I can have the sheriff here pretty quickly, and he isn't going to look kindly on game rigging." He set down the cork gun and stepped back as the operator swore under his breath and went through the process of closing up.

"Thanks, mister," one of the kids said, carrying a huge Pikachu that he could barely see over the top of.

"You're welcome." Hilliard smiled as the kids walked away, hopefully to find their shocked parents. "Sorry about that."

Brian chuckled. "You just can't help it, can you?"

"What?"

"Do you take up every cause that crosses your path? Mine, the waitresses when we were out, those kids being cheated. You just have to help."

Hilliard shrugged. "I became a lawyer to help others. It wasn't for the money. I wanted to try to do good in the world, to help people who others wouldn't. I sort of lost track of that the past few years. I was in Ohio. Alan and I got absorbed in building the practice. He used to tell me that we could help people once we built our reputation." The more he thought about it, the more he realized that Alan cheating and eventually buying him out was the best thing that could have happened to him. If that hadn't happened, he probably would have lost who he was completely and ended up as heartless and cold as Alan.

"You know that's just cover for being selfish. Alan didn't want to help anyone other than himself. He was a selfish jerk. Cheating on someone proves that." Brian took his hand. "Come on. I want to play the candy game. It may not have skill, but it's a lot of fun." He pulled them over to a booth with four sides divided into colored squares. "Put a buck on the color you think is going to win. Someone throws the ball in the center, and if it lands on your color, you win." Brian was so excited that Hilliard found himself fishing out some money.

"YOU'RE TOO danged lucky," Brian groused good-naturedly when Hilliard won for the fourth time. Granted, Brian had won twice, and between them they had a pile of bags of peanut butter cups and M&M's.

"I'll share with you," Hilliard said with a wink, lightly bumping Brian's shoulder. All the drama from earlier seemed to have slipped away as they played and laughed, teasing each other as they either won or lost.

"Okay, then." Brian gathered their prizes and stepped back from the game. "Let's get out of here before I'm tempted to break out more money to see if I can catch up." They laughed as they headed away from the game and walked through the grounds. "We should check on Gran." Brian led back to where they'd left her and found Beverly holding court with half a dozen ladies all riveted as she told stories—a group that included Violet Trainer.

"Well, look at that," Hilliard said.

"They all flock to her. No one can stay mad at Gran for long," Brian said. "Gran… are you okay?"

"I'm fine, but we could all use another round." Clearly the ladies had moved on from tea to wine. "Could you go get some? We need three pinots, a chardonnay, and two rieslings." She patted Brian's hand, and he came up with a few bills. Brian headed away to get what she needed, and Beverly pointed to another chair that Hilliard pulled over to sit next to her.

"I'm told you're making progress," Violet said, finishing the last of her wine.

"I think so. Would it be okay if we came to see you tomorrow? I have a few questions that you might be able to answer."

She nodded seriously, pursing her lips. "Do you think it was part of my family?"

Hilliard wasn't sure how to answer. "I'm not sure, but my gut is telling me that it isn't." Well, that and his eavesdropping, but he was also being honest.

Violet seemed somewhat reassured. "Okay. I'll hold on to that."

"Don't worry. Hilliard is smart, and he'll figure it out." Beverly patted her hand. "After all, what we all want is the truth."

"Yes. That we all do." She waited as Brian returned with a tray and glasses. He set it down, and Beverly passed out the various drinks.

"Thank you," Beverly told Brian with a wink. "Now, Violet dear, do you think that you could arrange for Hilliard to talk to Kevin and Kendall?"

She set down her glass. "But you said…."

"I don't think your grandsons would steal from you," Hilliard clarified. "But they may have some information we can use. I'm not going to give them the third degree, and you can be there when I talk to them. But I need to hear what they have to say. I'll even bring some coffee and doughnuts." No one could be angry at that—he hoped.

"All right. Stop by tomorrow at ten," Violet said before sipping from her wineglass.

"All you ladies have a good time." Hilliard stood and led Brian away. Clearly the ladies had settled in for an evening of wine and gossip. They didn't need him and Brian getting in the way. "What do we do next?"

"The Ferris wheel?" Brian asked, leading him over. Hilliard bought tickets, and they got in line.

The wheel wasn't very big, but this close to the ocean, it didn't need to be in order to provide a great view. As they rode toward the top, the entire town fanned out below them, then beyond that, the ocean, growing darker, lightened in places by the waves crashing against the rocks. As they came back to earth, the view faded, only to return as they made their ascent.

"I thought about leaving," Brian said, shifting closer in the cooling night air. The clouds formed a roof above them, and at the wheel's height, Hilliard almost felt like he could reach out and touch them. He tugged Brian closer, sharing his warmth as they continued their ride. "After I got out, I really thought about going to the city to try to escape. I probably could have hidden my past there and done better."

"Why didn't you?" Hilliard asked.

"Gran… and this is my home. I knew I didn't do it. And I guess I was hoping that someone would believe me. Gran always did." Brian turned toward him, and Hilliard leaned in closer. "Then this lawyer comes to town, and suddenly everything changed." He smiled, and Hilliard kissed him lightly just as they crested the top. "I don't know how you did it. I can't believe Violet is having us over tomorrow, or…." His voice grew rough.

"Violet wants the thief caught, and she wants to get her things back, but that isn't likely to happen. Most stolen goods are fenced and sold off in a matter of days. I doubt it's that hard to do…." As soon as the words crossed his lips, he saw the fault in his logic.

"What is it?"

"The damned napkin holder," he said softly. "What the hell was it doing there?" Their ride came to an end, and Hilliard got off and hurried to a quiet place. "I've been looking at this all wrong. A thief isn't going to hold on to what they stole for any longer than they have to. They'd break in, steal the goods, and sell them for what they could get as fast as possible." He hugged Brian as he had a moment of clarity. "So why would the thief keep a damned napkin ring just hanging around all this time? As evidence to place just in case someone came sniffing around two years later? No damned way." His spine tingled, and he knew he was onto something, but he wasn't quite sure what.

"You think the thief stole something else just to place it in my things?"

Then it hit him. "*Someone* did." A picture was just starting to emerge. He needed some more information, but it was there. Still blurry and fuzzy around the edges, but parts of it were becoming clear. With just a little more information, he might have everything he needed. He stood still, willing more pieces to fall into place, but it just wasn't happening. Not yet, anyway, but it would. Hilliard was sure of it.

Chapter 14

Gran was sleeping off her wine. Ruth said she'd had three glasses. As soon as Brian had gotten her home and in bed, the dogs took up their places on either side of her, and now she was snoring like a sailor. Occasionally the dogs lifted their heads to see what the racket was before putting them down again. Brian partially closed the door and went downstairs.

"Do you want to go to my place?" Hilliard asked.

Brian wanted nothing more. "I can't. She had a lot of wine, and what if something happens?" He sat on Gran's sofa, and Hilliard moved from the chair to sit next to him.

"I understand." He smiled and nudged against Brian. Before he knew it, Hilliard leaned in, kissing him gently at first, but adding pressure. Brian held on to him, holding Hilliard as he pressed him down against the cushions, the energy between them crackling like a live wire. Brian felt like he was on fire, he needed more so badly. He had spent the entire evening thinking about Hilliard. At one point he had stretched, and it took all Brian's willpower not to caress that strip of honey skin along his belly. Not that Hilliard did anything on purpose, but still, Brian's fingers had ached to touch, and he had to keep reminding himself that they weren't in Hilliard's bedroom.

"We should stop," Brian whispered when he took a breath. He sat up, straightening his clothes. "We really can't do this here." He felt himself coloring.

"Why not? Your grandmother is asleep, and she isn't waking up any time soon."

Brian rolled his eyes. "I'm not going to make out with you on my grandmother's sofa. I'm not a teenager, and I feel like I'm doing something naughty."

"No problem." Hilliard slipped down onto the floor and pulled Brian right along with him. He grinned and ran his fingers over Brian's cheek, drawing him closer. "Are you feeling less naughty now? Because

I can make you forget everything except your name if you let me. But now isn't the time for that."

Brian quivered as Hilliard kissed him, gently, carefully, like he was something special. Kissing Hilliard was always an amazing experience. Brian's body seemed to know what it wanted and reacted to him within seconds, and this time was no exception, but Hilliard didn't deepen the kiss or press him down onto the floor. Instead, he held him, kissing gently, leaving Brian breathless and a little confused. "You know, you're right. Now isn't the time to make love—it's the time to *be* loved." Hilliard stroked his cheek and then got up to turn out the lights. Once the room was dark, he shimmied behind him and held Brian between his legs. Hillard wrapped his arms around him and tugged Brian against his chest.

He sighed when Hilliard didn't move, just holding Brian in his arms. He relaxed and lolled his head back, letting go of the tension that was his constant companion. "Do you really think we'll be able to unravel this mystery?"

"Yes," Hilliard breathed softly.

"I just want this over and to put it all behind me." Brian sighed. "God, this feels good." He turned slightly. "I always thought that being with someone…." Suddenly he didn't have words that didn't sound stupid.

"Would be about nothing but sex?" Hilliard asked. Brian nodded. "A relationship is about more than that." He held him a little tighter. "Though I didn't know that when I went into my last one."

"What was Alan like? I know he's an asshole, but I'm assuming he wasn't always that way." He really wanted to know.

For a moment Hilliard grew quiet. "I think at the beginning I was attracted to his confidence. Alan always seemed to have these visions of what was possible, and then he made them happen. It was kind of sexy watching him bend the world to his way of thinking. And he was a man of action, both in law school and afterwards. He got both of us prime positions, and we made names for ourselves. I always thought he was looking out for both of us." Hilliard released him with one hand. Brian took it and held it. "But I see now that it was all for him. He did things because he thought he was going to benefit from them. We had good résumés and were well trained and bright. We started our own firm and we beat the bushes. I thought we were happy and had it all, but Alan wanted more."

Hilliard tensed, and Brian wished he could see him. "I know I told you I caught him cheating, but I turned a blind eye to it. I was such a fool." He shivered, and Brian moved out of his embrace, knelt in front of him, and held Hilliard's watery gaze. "I thought if I were better or if I gave him more of what he wanted then everything would be great. But he simply took and went on as before as long as he got what he wanted. The firm was doing well, and…."

Brian got it. "He didn't need you anymore."

"He just bought me out, and I haven't heard another word from him. And I probably never will again." He lowered his gaze. "I was just something he could throw away." Hilliard shrugged.

"Then he's an idiot. Because anyone who would do that is a complete jerk. I know it's still raw, but I don't treat people like that. I've been on the other end, so I know how it feels." He wished he could do something to help.

"I know that I come off as confident and decisive, but it's so easy to believe the worst."

"Tell me about it," Brian said softly. "But we have to do our best to silence those voices. The put-downers are just people who want something from us. They want control." He leaned closer. "Good people don't take advantage, and they don't tear you down to build themselves up. Those people really suck."

"And not in a good way," Hilliard added.

Brian smiled at his moment of levity. "No. We have to put their crap out of our heads and trust in ourselves. You can do whatever you set your mind to, I know that. Alan is a real loser, and I bet he's going to find out that it isn't so easy to do things on his own. And once people find out what he's really like, there won't be others who will want to work for him. He'll get what's coming to him. You called him a shark? Well, they have a tendency to eat the other fish, even their own kind." Brian held Hilliard's gaze. He loved looking into those deep eyes, wishing he knew more of what he was thinking. "I do have to say one thing, though. If you stay here, you are not likely to ever see him again or end up in a courtroom with him."

Hilliard hugged him, chuckling as tears ran down both their cheeks. "You chose this moment to make your case?"

Brian held him tighter. "I don't have that much ammunition, so I keep my powder dry and only use it when I think it will do the most good. I'm a handyman who is trying to clear his name, and you're a lawyer who could work just about anywhere. I need to make my shots count."

Hilliard pulled back. "No, you don't. You just have to be honest and tell me how you feel."

Brian nodded. "Then I want you to stay, but not just for me. I want you to keep your great-aunt's house, live there, and build a life here. I want you to be happy, and I want us to have a chance. So if I'm spelling it out, that's it. I know it sounds like a lot, but it's what I hope will happen." He sighed because he had never spelled things out like that. It seemed like whenever he let himself hope for something good, it went to hell.

"Then I guess I have to figure out how to make that happen. Starting over is hard, but I think trying to return to Ohio would be worse. I have everything I need here, and while I don't know if there is enough work here to sustain a practice…."

"There is. Gran said that there used to be a number of lawyers in town, but they either moved or passed away. People here have money, and if you earn their loyalty and have a sound reputation, they will support you, I know it." He cleared his throat. "I'm getting more work now than I ever have, and they're willing to forgive my somewhat checkered past." He wiped his cheeks.

"Okay. I'll do my best," Hilliard said. "There are a lot of things I need to do before I can open shop, so we'll have to take things one step at a time."

"I think I can live with that," Brian whispered. The last thing he wanted to do was try to extract a firmer commitment from Hilliard. He had never given Brian a cause to doubt him, so he'd take him at his word. He leaned closer, holding him hard, letting himself savor the moment, hoping that everything worked out the way they both hoped.

"THAT OLD shit," Hilliard said as soon as he answered Brian's phone call the following morning.

"Excuse me?" Brian wondered what that was about.

"Sorry. My uncle. He served me with papers last night when I got home. They were waiting when I got back. It seems he's trying to challenge the will."

"Can he do that?" Brian asked.

Hilliard humphed. "He can try, but it isn't going anywhere. The man is a bully, and this is just one of his tactics. I'm willing to bet that he's looking for something to make him go away. But it takes a lot to mount a successful challenge, and his claim doesn't meet that level—quite far from it."

"And let me guess: you were up half the night researching standards and reviewing the will to make sure that your case was solid." He expected that Hilliard didn't get to sleep until the wee hours of the morning.

"Yeah, kinda. I left a message with my aunt's attorney so he would know what was going on."

"I was going to ask if you wanted to have breakfast and talk things over before we go to Violet's later, but maybe this isn't such a good time."

"No, it's fine. I have a few things to do. But I'll meet you there." Hilliard disconnected, and Brian set down his phone as Gran came in, moving slowly.

"Don't talk to me. Whatever they put in that wine was evil," Gran said. Brian snickered softly. "Don't give me any of that, young man. I took one for the cause and got Violet to play nice. Just because she now knows you didn't rob her doesn't mean that she's your best friend or anything." She sat down, and Brian brought her a mug of coffee. "Damn, I'm going to put you up for sainthood for this." She sipped and closed her eyes. "Remind me to never do that again."

"You had some wine and you slept all night. You should be ready for another bender," he teased.

Gran glared at him for a second but wasn't able to hold it. She groaned before sipping a little more coffee. "Is Hilliard coming for breakfast?"

"No. He has an issue of his own that he's working through. He'll meet me at Violet's." He sipped his own coffee and wished there was a way he could help. Not that he knew anything about wills. Maybe the best thing he could do was to leave Hilliard alone. "Timothy is challenging the will, and Hilliard was notified last night. I think this really has him thrown."

Gran lifted her gaze from the table. "Then get dressed, make some breakfast, and take it over to him."

"He's busy, and—"

She sighed. "I'm not hungry, and I need some quiet with my coffee before I'll feel like anything other than the walking dead. In the meantime, he needs your support. I know you can't do anything to make this go away, but you can be there for him." She drummed the table with her fingers and then stopped and clamped her eyes shut. "Just trust me. Be there for the good and the crap. That's what you do when you care about someone."

Brian knew she was right. He stood and slipped on his shoes as he headed for the door.

"Sweetheart, you might want to put on something other than what you were sleeping in."

Brian looked down, sighed, and hurried upstairs to change his clothes.

"I THOUGHT we were going to meet at Violet's," Hilliard said when he answered the door.

"Poppy and Gigi needed a walk, and I figured you would need breakfast and maybe some coffee." Brian wrinkled his nose. "And maybe a shower?"

Hilliard sniffed and made a face of his own. "I think you're right." He stepped back, and Brian brought the dogs inside. They immediately made themselves at home, exploring the room before settling together on the sofa, watching the humans as though there was going to be a show. "I'm going to clean up. There's nothing more I can do about the will right now anyway. I got a message that the lawyer wants to meet on Monday, but he says Timothy doesn't have a leg to stand on and he'll draw up a response." Hilliard didn't sound convinced.

"What has you worried?" Brian stood in front of him as Hilliard bit his lower lip.

"I don't know. The things Timothy alleges in his argument aren't true, and it sounds like a self-entitled rant, but…."

Brian shrugged. "He got you thinking."

Hilliard drew closer. "Actually, what he did was help clarify things for me. Aunt Grace was very specific in her will, and she left Timothy some money, so she made her wishes clear. No doubt about that."

"Then what do you do?"

"I'm going to fight him. I have fond memories with Aunt Grace, and Uncle Timothy has to be a real loser if his own mother cut him out of her will. I had nothing to do with that. The only contact I had with her was the cards she sent me at the holidays and the ones I sent her. That's about it."

"I see." Did that mean that Hilliard was staying? Hilliard had said that he was. But maybe this fight with his uncle would have him rethinking his plans.

Hilliard smiled. "I need to clean up quick. I'll be right back." He headed upstairs, and Brian sat on the sofa next to the dogs, wondering if coming here was a good idea. Maybe he should have just met him at Violet's.

Brian huffed, and Gigi climbed into his lap. He stroked her, looking upward the stairs. The water came on, and Brian gently moved the dog away, then went up, following the sound of the water before gently knocking on the door. "Hilliard…?" He swallowed hard, wondering if this was too forward.

The door opened to Hilliard in only a towel. "Is something wrong?"

Brian cupped Hilliard's face in his hands. "I thought you might be lonely." He kissed him hard, and Hilliard drew Brian into the bathroom and closed the door.

"I was a little." Hilliard dropped the towel and stepped under the spray.

Brian slipped out of his clothes and joined him. "You know, we're supposed to conserve water, and I haven't had my shower yet today." He pulled the curtain closed behind him and pressed against Hilliard's back.

"So that's what this is—you came this entire way to save water?" He turned around, tugging Brian to him. "How ecologically responsible of you. Maybe you should be rewarded for your thoughtfulness." He winked and sank down, taking Brian's cock between his lips in a single motion.

"Oh God," Brian whimpered. Clamping his eyes closed, he let the sensation wash over him, because… damn. He backed up slightly, pressing to the tile, using the cool, hard surface to keep upright as Hilliard played him like a fine instrument. When Hilliard took him the whole way, all Brian could do was groan and hold on as Hilliard's water-slick head bobbed in front of him. "Hill… I'm…," he warned as he tried to control his errant body. Hilliard seemed more in control of him than he was, and didn't stop, sucking harder until Brian lost it completely, shooting down Hilliard's throat as he leaned against the wall, hoping he didn't end up on the floor of the tub in a heap.

He breathed deeply as Hilliard made soft noises, and Brian looked down just as Hilliard climaxed below him.

Brian gently lifted him back to his feet and reached for the soap, rubbing it between his hands before slicking Hilliard's chest and then his shoulders and arms before letting his hands slip down to the really interesting bits.

"If you're trying to raise an interest, I think it's a little soon again, but if you give me time…."

Brian grinned. "I think I'm just making sure everything gets a good wash." He patted Hilliard's hip, and he turned around. Brian slicked his hands again and soaped his back and down over Hilliard's perfect firm bubble butt.

"I see. And do I get to return the favor?"

"I'd hope you'd want to." He slipped his fingers between Hilliard's legs and then up his back again before finishing at his shoulders. Brian let him rinse off and then stepped under the spray so Hilliard could wash him.

He closed his eyes, letting the warm water run down his back as Hilliard soaped his front, breath hitching as he stroked his awakening cock. When he turned around, Hilliard soaped his back and then pressed to him, his hard cock sliding along the crease of his ass. "Didn't take long."

"Not with you," Hilliard whispered and pressed them both forward, the water sending the soap down the drain. Hilliard turned off the water and got them both towels. "I'd really like to spend the next couple hours finishing what we started."

Brian sighed. "I know. But we need to get dressed and go to Violet's."

Hilliard kissed him. "Yeah. We need to keep our minds clear, and right now, you are one hell of a distraction." He left the room, and Brian got dressed. Then he met Hilliard downstairs, where they had a quick breakfast. The man still looked edible in jeans that hugged his ass and a T-shirt that showed off his arms. Brian was tempted to try to lure Hilliard into staying a little longer, but they were expected. And who knew? They might actually figure something out about the burglary.

Chapter 15

"How is Beverly after last night?" Hilliard asked as he and Brian walked over to Violet's mini mansion in the center of town. Hilliard carried a case of papers that held the information he'd gathered. They'd left the dogs at Hilliard's house, both of them curled up on the sofa.

"She was a little under the weather, and I suspect that once I left and she'd finished her coffee, she probably sat in her chair and fell back to sleep."

"Okay. So not really any worse for wear, then. I was a little worried with the way she was downing the wine."

They approached the house, opened the gate, and headed up the walk before ringing the bell. Violet answered the door and led them through to the impeccable dining room with a table large enough for twelve. On one side sat the two boys, their attention on their phones.

"Kendall and Kevin, this is Hilliard, and he's trying to figure out who broke into my house." She met both their gazes.

"We didn't do it," they said in unison. "I thought he did," Kendall said, pointing at Brian.

"He was at the Point Cabrillo Light when your grandmother was robbed, and we can prove it. So Brian is not the thief." Hilliard sat down across from them.

"Well, it wasn't us," Kevin said softly. "We would never rob Grandma. Have you seen her when she's angry? She's scary as sh…. She's scary." They looked at each other and then back at Hilliard.

"Maybe you didn't. But why should anyone believe you? You made a mess of my car because you thought it was fun, and I've seen you in town, racing down streets and riding on the sidewalk, nearly hitting people." And that was just the past few weeks. "You don't have the best record of behavior."

"Grandma, we never—" Kevin started, almost pleading, his expression pained.

"Yeah," Kendall added. The boys looked about seventeen but sounded a lot younger.

"Okay, boys," Violet said. "I believe you. But you have to tell Mr. Hilliard here everything you know and answer his questions." She sat down. "Someone came into my house and took things that were important to me." She was clearly playing on their emotions, and it was working, because they lowered their heads.

"We know, Grandma. It was really gross."

"Okay, boys, there's something you need to know. Whoever robbed your grandmother knew where her things were kept. They came in, took them, and didn't even have to look. They already knew." Hilliard watched both boys. "Did your grandmother ever tell you where she kept valuable things?"

He glanced at Violet, who nodded slowly; then he shifted his gaze to the boys, who looked straight ahead and didn't answer.

"Kevin and Kendall," Brian said softly, "we are trying to see if we can get your grandmother's things back. Helping us is going to help your grandma too."

"Yeah," Kevin finally said. "I knew where Grandma kept stuff. She showed me once, but I never went in there and took it. Like I want to touch grandma underwear." Hilliard almost chuckled but held it together. "Kendall knew too."

"Did you ever tell anyone?" Hilliard asked. Both boys looked at each other like that was a completely foreign thought before they shook their heads. "Do you know who robbed your grandmother?" He got another head shake. "But you think you do."

Kendall pushed the chair back and stalked out of the room while Kevin stared down at the table, his shoulders shaking. "Dad."

Violet seemed shocked, but Hilliard shook his head at her. "Why do you think that?" Kevin shrugged, and Hilliard waited. Kendall returned and sat back down. Clearly he'd been listening.

"I saw him with a piece of jewelry. He was putting it in his pocket. But I don't know if it was Grandma's."

Hilliard pulled out his case and withdrew the picture of the necklace that had been found in Brian's truck. "Is that what you saw?" He showed Kendall the picture, and he nodded. Hilliard also showed the picture to Violet, who got up and left the room, wiping her eyes.

Kevin nodded. "Yeah. Then I never saw it again."

Violet returned with a shiny wooden box and set it on the table. "That wasn't with the other items. It was in here." She sat down.

Hilliard's head began to spin. "So that wasn't taken as part of the burglary?" Just when he thought he was coming to the end of this mystery, something else popped up. Tension washed off Brian, and he knew he was feeling the same frustration. Yet Hilliard knew they were getting close. Maybe the puzzle wasn't as simple as he'd first thought, but the answer was closer. Hilliard squeezed Brian's leg under the table to try to reassure him.

"It may have been, but why? My husband gave me that when we were on our honeymoon. The stone was big, but it was only agate and not monetarily valuable. I kept it in here."

Hilliard stilled and then reached into his bag to pull out the police report. He went through it again and swore under his breath before pointing to a line and showing it to Brian. It seemed they had their answer, about that at least. "Tell us again where you were when your grandma was robbed." Hilliard didn't want to lose momentum.

"We were…," Kendall began, looking at Kevin. Hilliard instantly knew what they'd said before was a lie.

"Remember, this is to help your grandma." He wasn't above twisting the knife.

Kevin nudged Kendall, who seemed to be wavering.

"We know you were lying, so tell us the truth now." He wasn't going to let them off, not for a second, and saw their resolve falter right before his eyes.

"We got a six-pack of beer and…," Kendall said quietly. "Kevin drank most of it."

"I did not," Kevin argued, the boys bickering back and forth.

"And it was just the two of you?" Hilliard asked, a clearer picture coming into focus. Both boys nodded, then hung their heads. "And you're sure you never told anyone where your grandma kept things?" He might as well go for broke. The boys looked at each other, and suddenly neither of them was as sure as they had been earlier. Finally each of them shrugged. Hilliard had been young once and knew how boys liked to brag, and that would be all it took.

"Thank you both," Hilliard said gently. "I think you've been a big help to your grandmother."

"We can go now?" Kendall asked.

"Yes," Violet said and held out her hands. The boys hurried over and each gave her a hug. As she held them, the front door opened and slammed closed.

"What is going on here?" Frank's voice boomed through the house. The boys stiffened and paled. Violet's eyes hardened just as Frank barreled into the room. "I heard that he was questioning my sons."

"That's quite enough of your blustering, Frankie. Sit down." Damn, Violet had snap, and she wasn't afraid to use it. "Boys, you can go, but I want to talk to both of you tonight."

"Yes," they each said as they hurried out of the room like the hounds of hell were after them.

"What's the meaning of this?" Frank demanded, standing at the edge of the table, looming over it.

"Sit down!" Violet snapped. "You have some explaining to do." She grabbed the photograph copy off the table and sent it sailing toward Frank. "You thieving little piece of shit." She vibrated with rage as she stood, the two of them glaring at each other down the long table. "I've done everything for you all your life and you steal from me?"

Frank lifted the page and set it down once more, swallowing hard before steeling himself.

"You were seen with that by your son. He just told us." Violet looked like she was about to explode, and Hilliard took her hand. She squeezed it, and Hilliard winced at the pressure.

"I didn't break in here and steal your things," Frank said smugly. "And I was with friends then. The police talked to me, and I not only had an alibi, but so did my boys. So whatever these two are peddling is pond scum."

"It's okay, Violet. I've got it from here," Hilliard said. He smiled at her, hoping she'd calm down and relax. He didn't want her hurting herself, because if he was right, those boys were going to need her. "So I think it's time for you to cut the bullshit. I know you're involved in this. Did you rob your own mother?" He couldn't keep the look of distaste from his face. "What kind of man are you?"

If Frank's head grew any redder, it might burst into flame. "Of course I didn't."

Hilliard leaned forward. "Then why did you frame Brian for it?" At least this piece of the picture was clear. "You took this piece of jewelry from your mother, and you placed it in Brian's truck. Then, when the police came to verify it, *you* confirmed that it was one of the pieces stolen. Not your mother." He passed the report from the police to Brian.

"You didn't," Violet said gently, her hand in front of her mouth. "Why would you do that?" She stood. "Why?" she yelled, her voice carrying through the entire house and, Hilliard expected, clear out into the street. "Tell me! Why would you do that?"

Frank held his posture straight for a few more seconds before his shoulders slumped. "I was protecting my family. When I heard about the burglary, I knew that Kevin and Kendall had been out with those friends of theirs, and…." He swallowed.

"You thought the boys were involved in the burglary and you took matters into your own hands. You planted evidence in Brian's truck in order to implicate him." Hilliard stood and leaned over the table. "You picked as your victim a man who was grieving the loss of his grandfather?" He shook his head and held Frank's gaze and saw fear filling his eyes. "And let me guess, you broke into Beverly's house to plant the napkin ring to try to throw renewed suspicion on him."

Frank hung his head, defeated. "I had to do something…."

"You thought the police would arrest him again? They can't. Double jeopardy. That was your biggest mistake. You overplayed your hand."

Brian had his phone out and left the room. Hilliard knew he was calling the police. At least with this, they had enough to vacate the conviction. All Hilliard needed to do was find a local attorney to act as sponsor and he could submit the paperwork to vacate the conviction on the grounds of new evidence. It would take time to get a court date, but they had more than enough to clear Brian.

"I…."

Violet stood still, shaking, and Hilliard helped her sit down. Frank stood and looked like he was going to leave. "Stay here. The police are probably on their way, and after what I have to tell them, they would only hunt you down anyway. It would probably be best if you went willingly."

Brian returned, and once Frank sat again, Hilliard went out into the hall with him. "Grant is on his way."

"Good." Hilliard smiled, and Brian hugged the life out of him.

"I didn't think this was possible," Brian whispered. "After everything." He shook in Hilliard's arms for a while. "I want to beat the living hell out of him for what he did to me."

"I know" was all Hilliard could say. "But you can't. He'll pay for what he did in so many ways." He would make sure of that. "Why don't you go wait for the police? You don't need to see him if you don't want to." Hilliard gave him another squeeze and then backed away. He wanted to stay with Brian, but it was best if Brian wasn't with Frank right now.

"What else was I going to do? I had to protect the boys," Frank was saying.

"Except I don't think they had anything to do with this," Hilliard told him. "Your sons would never hurt their grandmother. I'm willing to bet that she is the only good thing in their lives. You, on the other hand, don't care who you hurt." He drew closer. "And now you've ruined Brian's life, as well as your own and the boys', because they are going to spend quite a bit of time without a father and your sorry ass is going to be in jail. Beverly and Brian will press charges for breaking and entering. You broke into Brian's truck, planted evidence, and framed an innocent man." He smiled. "And I suspect that Brian will bring a civil suit and can easily take every cent you have or will ever have."

Frank paled, and for a second Hilliard thought he might pass out.

"Is it really that bad?" Violet asked.

"I'm afraid so. He stole years from a man's life. Someone who was innocent all along." Hilliard was so angry on Brian's behalf that he wanted to lash out at Frank—and at Violet for taking his side, but then, Frank was her son, and just like Brian had Beverly, Frank was going to need someone in his corner.

A firm knock pulled him away, and he opened the front door to let Grant and a deputy inside. Hilliard gave Grant a brief recap.

"And he admitted all this?"

"In front of myself, Brian, and his mother. Also, I found a few gems in the police report that will back up the story." Hilliard gave Grant the entire breakdown.

"But he isn't the thief," Grant said.

"No. He's just Brian's framer—and I think that's the worse of the crimes. Sure, someone stole Violet's things, but Frank stole part of Brian's life."

Grant nodded. "We'll take it from here, and we'll need you all to give a statement."

"Gladly." Hilliard followed Grant into the dining room, and he cuffed Frank and read him his rights. Then Hilliard followed them out and joined Brian on the porch. "At least part of it is over." Brian nodded and pulled out his phone. "What are you doing?"

"Taking pictures of the asshole who framed me." He snapped some images of Frank in cuffs and then put his phone away. Brian shook next to him, and Hilliard put an arm around him, drawing him close. Hilliard turned to look at him just as Brian buried his face in Hilliard's shirt… and began to cry. Years of hurt and shame seemed to come to the surface all at once, and Hilliard didn't blame Brian at all. Hell, he wondered how Brian had kept it together for as long as he had.

"It's going to be okay now. All the evidence against you is slowly slipping away."

"It's not that," Brian said.

Hilliard expected an explanation, but Brian clammed up. "Let's go home," he said gently.

Brian shook his head. "I have to make sure Violet is all right." He went back inside, wiping his face. Hilliard stayed where he was until the police pulled away, then joined Brian, finding him and Violet at the dining room table, each holding the other's hands, sharing their loss and shock, both likely feeling the exact same thing over the same situation, but for opposite reasons.

Hilliard stepped out of the room. "Ruth, it's Hilliard," he said when she answered the call.

"Yes, honey?" she said softly.

"Can you come to Violet's? She's had a bit of a shock, and I don't think she should be alone. Brian and I are here, but I need to take him home."

"Of course I can. But why?" she asked.

"We didn't find the thief, but her son Frank confessed to framing Brian because he thought his sons were the thieves. It's an emotional minefield."

Ruth gasped. "I'll be there as soon as I can. Don't worry. The ladies will see that Violet gets the support she needs." She hung up, and Hilliard went back inside. Tears ran down Violet's cheeks.

"It's okay," Brian said, looking at Hilliard like he wasn't sure what to do.

"Ruth will be over in a few minutes," Hilliard said softly. "We'll wait until she gets here." He didn't want to leave Violet alone, so he pulled out a chair and sat down until he heard a knock at the door. He let Ruth in, and she took over like the force of nature she was.

Hilliard got Brian out of the house, and they walked back to Hilliard's. Poppy and Gigi crowded around Brian as soon as he sat down. They must have known that he needed them. Poppy stretched up and licked his ear as Gigi hopped into his lap. Hilliard made some coffee. When he returned to the living room, the dogs had found a way to curl around Brian, whose head rested back against the sofa cushion.

"I thought at this moment I'd be happy. That I could smile and laugh because finally I've gotten what I wanted. Everyone will know that I'm not a thief, and…."

Hilliard gently sat next to him, getting a soft growl from Gigi. Brian lightly scolded her, and she licked his hand as an apology. "The important people already knew that." He smiled and rested his head on Brian's shoulder.

"I know that. Gran never stopped believing. But what I don't get is why you believed me in the first place."

Hilliard thought for a few seconds before trying to answer. "I don't know. I'd like to say it was because of some innate lie-detecting ability or the way you looked at me, but the truth is, I just knew. I've done quite a bit of thinking, and that's the best I can come up with. I'm an experienced attorney, and I've heard enough bullshit to last a lifetime, but I knew that what I was getting from you was the truth." He drew Brian closer and kissed him hard, pouring all the relief and joy he felt into it.

When Brian shifted nearer, the dogs jumped down. "I'm glad you did, for so many reasons."

The dogs barked, which was unusual. Brian stiffened and pulled away. Hilliard went out front but didn't see anyone. "Maybe we should get them home. Your grandmother is going to want to know what we found out too."

"Yeah," Brian agreed, his eyes filling with disappointment. "Maybe we can get together later."

"To celebrate, definitely." Hilliard kissed Brian and helped him get the leashes on the dogs; then he said goodbye at the door and watched them go. He waved a final time and closed the door before going up to his office. He had some work to do and phone calls to make to get the ball rolling from a legal perspective. Since he wasn't licensed to practice yet, he needed someone to act as a sponsor—to act as lead while he did the work. And he set about the job of trying to locate someone willing to help.

Chapter 16

"GRAN?" BRIAN called as he went inside. He let the dogs off their leashes, and they hurried through the house. Gigi's sharp bark drew him upstairs. "Gran!" he said when he found her on her bedroom floor.

"What?" she asked as he lifted her head.

"You fell?" he asked.

"Yes," she breathed. "I didn't break anything, but when I sat up I felt dizzy, so I lay back down and must have fallen asleep. Help me up."

"Do you think that's a good idea? Maybe I should call an ambulance." His heart pounded. He didn't want her hurt.

"I'm okay. Just help me up." She sat up, and Brian helped her to her feet. She sat on the side of the bed, breathing deeply, the dogs both jumping up to make sure she was okay. "I didn't break anything, and I didn't hit my head. I was just a little dizzy and figured you'd be home soon enough." He got her settled on the bed and called Hilliard. Once he explained what happened, he was there within what seemed like seconds.

"Are you sure you're okay?" Hilliard asked her, and then asked Gran basic questions.

"I'm fine. I know what year it is and where I am. I just fell down and felt dizzy, so I stayed there." She seemed annoyed. "I could use some tea, though."

"I'll go make it," Hilliard offered, and he left the room.

"That man is a keeper," Gran said once Hilliard was gone. "He's kind, and he cares for you."

Brian sighed. "I know he does."

Gran took his hand. "I'm not going to be around forever, and I want to know that you aren't going to be alone. I want you to be happy, and I want you to have your life back." She glanced toward the door. "Which it seems Hilliard has made possible, from what I understand."

"I guess. We still don't know who committed the burglary," Brian said.

"That doesn't matter. There is a confession for who framed you, and that should be enough, with the alibi, to get you off the hook. And that was the goal—to find out the truth and clear your name." Brian smiled slightly. "So why are you so worried?"

"I don't know. Hilliard's uncle is giving him a hard time about the estate, and I keep wondering if he's going to wake up and realize that his life would be a lot easier and quieter back in Cleveland."

Gran chuckled. "Please. Who wants quiet and easy… especially in Cleveland? Has he said anything about what he is going to do?"

"Well, I think he wants to stay, I really do, but…."

"Then maybe the two of you need to talk things over. Tell him what you want. You know you have a right to what will make you happy. Let him know how you feel." Gran tugged him closer. "There are few things more attractive and sexy than a man who knows what he wants and is willing to put his heart out there." She cleared her throat as Hilliard returned with a mug of hot tea and set it on the bedside table.

"Is there anything more that you'd like?" Hilliard asked.

"No. I'm fine. Why don't the two of you go on downstairs? I'll be fine." She lifted the mug by the handle and sipped slowly. "I'm fine, really. Don't go turning into a couple of worrywarts. I'm not quite ready to cross the bridge into the great beyond—not yet." She shooed them out of the room. The dogs stayed with her on the bed, though.

"What was all that about?" Hilliard asked once they were downstairs.

"Gran is worried that I think she's going to die." Brian sat on the sofa with Hilliard next to him. Brian scratched his head nervously. "I have something I want to say, but I don't know how to say it right. So I'll just say that I really want you to stay."

"I see." Hilliard smiled. "Is that all?" He cocked his eyebrows, and his lips quirked a little.

"For now," Brian said, "that will do. I may come up with more things that I want later. But I hope what I want is what you want. I guess that's the thing, right? Finding someone you care about who wants the same things you do."

Brian held Hilliard's gaze. He had put his cards on the table, and now it was up to Hilliard. Brian's belly did flip-flops, and he was almost afraid to breathe. Maybe he would have been better off to keep quiet. After all, if he didn't know the answer, then there was still hope. Still, maybe Gran was right and it was best to know.

"I know we've talked about this and that I've sent you a lot of mixed signals. So… yeah. I want that too. I have every intention of fighting my uncle, who doesn't have a leg to stand on anyway. His suit will likely be dismissed for lack of grounds. And I like it here. I like that I can start over and build a new life." Hilliard leaned closer. "That we can build a life together. I sort of feel like you're free now." He swallowed hard.

"And I owe you so much for that," Brian said.

Hilliard shook his head. "You owe me nothing. I don't want you to think that we're keeping score. What I did was because it was the right thing to do, and I'd do the same thing for anyone who asked for my help. And when you and I move forward, it will be because we both want to. No debts or anything like that." He drew closer. "I didn't help you because I thought you were sexy or because I wanted to get in your pants. I helped—"

"Because you just can't stop yourself," Brian interrupted with a smirk, caressing Hilliard's cheek.

"And I would have helped you even if you hadn't been the sexiest man ever to cross my path." Brian felt Hilliard's warm breath on his lips and saw the gold flecks dancing in his eyes. "I want to build a new life, and I want you to be part of it. I want to take you for drives up the coast and make love to the beat of the ocean as it pounds the rocks." His voice grew husky. "There are many things that I want to do, and when I close my eyes and think of them, I see us together."

"Like what?" Brian asked just loud enough to be heard. He swallowed hard.

"Maybe spring in Yosemite with the falls running full force, walking under trees that have been there for hundreds of years. Swimming in the Pacific, or in lakes warmed during the summer. I want to see all the west has to offer." He smiled. "Maybe spend the night in a tent where we're the only people for miles and all we see above is a curtain of stars."

Brian nodded. "I want that too."

Hilliard closed the distance between them, his lips touching Brian's in an electric shock that both made him jump and left him wanting more.

"I know you have to look after Beverly, but come to the house tonight if you can," Hilliard whispered. Brian nodded, and Hilliard kissed him again, harder and more urgently this time. "I have some things I need to get done, but I'll be waiting for you." He stood, first holding his hand, then letting his fingers gently slip away. Then he left, and Brian sat in the still room.

"Is everything okay?" Gran asked as she slowly came down the stairs, holding the railing. "From what I saw, it looked like it."

"Gran…." Brian sighed. "You don't need to be looking."

She shook her head. "Do I need to keep reminding you that I may be old, but I'm not dead? I'm feeling better, and Grant is taking me out to dinner this evening."

"Gran, you fell!" Brian was aghast.

"And I will hold his arm." She shrugged. "Oh, and try to find someplace to go this evening. After dinner, we're coming back here, and I'd like the chance to spend some time alone with him."

Brian tried not to appear shocked and upset. "Fine, Gran. Hilliard asked me to his place this evening." He stretched out his legs as she sat down in her chair.

"You look at loose ends," Gran said. "What's wrong? It seems like things are going well. You have someone who cares for you a great deal, and we've proven your innocence. I know it will take time for the conviction to be vacated, but it will happen."

"I know. I just…. We visited Violet, and she looked like part of her life had been ripped from her." He bit his lower lip. "I hate to see her so broken up. Frank really messed up, and the ass is going to jail, but…."

"You have a big heart," Gran said. "But Frank made his own bed when he did what he did."

"I know. But I keep wondering who the real thief is. I have some ideas of who it might be, but I don't know how to prove it or how I can even get close enough to talk to them." He was really frustrated.

Gran patted his hand. "That part of the case is the sheriff's job. The old case has completely fallen apart, and they know it. There are going to be prominent people calling to reopen the investigation, including Violet, I'm sure. This isn't how you and Hilliard should be spending your time." Her smile was the same one she used when he skinned a knee as a kid.

"Thanks, Gran," he said gently, hugging her before getting up. He had a job he needed to finish, so he hurried upstairs. After all this excitement, he could use a little quiet.

"I EMAILED Alan," Hilliard said once he and Brian sat down on Hilliard's back patio.

"What?" Brian asked, shocked.

"And then he called and we talked." He sipped his beer slowly as Brian watched him. "I needed a name from him, a contact of his from when we were in law school. I remembered that one of his friends back then had moved out here. He's a lawyer in San Francisco. Alan gave me his email address." He sighed. "And we talked a little." He turned to Brian, his eyes watering. "It was a kind of closure, I guess. There was no drama about him wanting me back or him saying he needed me. None of that stuff. He did say that he had messed up." Hilliard sipped from the bottle and sat back in the chair, looking up at the sky like he was talking to it. "As we talked, I realized that he and I wanted different things. Well, maybe at first we wanted the same thing, but for different reasons. Do you know what I mean?"

Brian wasn't sure, but he didn't want Hilliard to stop, so he nodded a little, more as encouragement than anything. "I suppose you wanted different things out of the firm?"

"Well, that… and each other, I guess. He wanted to be a shark, without a doubt, and I wanted to help people. For a while, that put us on the same path. But then… it didn't. I was softer I guess, quieter, and Alan wanted someone who…." He chuckled. "I guess I don't even know what I'm saying. He and I were on different paths, and for a long time they were close enough together that we thought it was just one, but I don't think it ever was. He said that he loved me and that he would never forget me, but…."

"That must have sucked."

"Not really. See, I loved him too, but I guess that had been fading for a while." Hilliard took his hand. "I know that things between him and me are over. They were even before I caught him cheating, and I can see that now. He has the firm, and he'll go forward with it. My name is off the door. And I'm going to open an office here just as soon as I can pass the bar. Until then, I'm going to get a job."

"I know a few places that are hiring," Brian told him.

Hilliard smiled. "I'm not going to work with you. I think that was part of my problem with Alan. We spent too much time together and didn't have a life that was separate." He leaned closer. "I don't want what happened to Alan and me to happen to us, so I'm going to see what I can find to make ends meet for a while until I can take the test. I already applied, and now I'm just waiting until they give it."

Brian smiled. "So you've definitely made up your mind."

"Yup. This is where I want to be." Hilliard finished his beer. Brian did the same, and then Hilliard stood, holding out his hand. Brian took it, and Hilliard led him inside and up the stairs into the bedroom.

The windows were open, and the power of the waves a hundred yards away, the wind across the open land, all of it swept inside. Hilliard wrapped him in strong arms and pressed him against the closed door with a thud. Brian's breath hitched and his eyes widened as Hilliard stared deeply into them. The panels of the door pressed to his back, but he ignored it. All that mattered was Hilliard's warmth. As he drew nearer, the intensity built until Hilliard took his lips in a bruising kiss that broke the dam holding Brian back.

He clutched Hilliard, grabbing his clothes in a desperate attempt to get at his skin. He needed him as badly as he needed air, and he was tired of waiting. They pulled apart only long enough to get their shirts off. Then they crashed together again, lips exploring as their hands did the same, tugging and pulling at belts and buttons before shoving pants aside.

Hilliard pushed them toward the bed, and they tumbled onto it in a fit of laughter, their pants around their ankles. Brian didn't care, and Hilliard didn't seem to either. They did manage to get their shoes off and kick their pants away, and Hilliard pressed Brian against the mattress, kissing him as though the world were going to end at any moment.

"Damn," Hilliard whispered between breaths. Brian cut him off with another kiss as Hilliard reached for the nightstand.

"I want you… fucking now." Brian groaned as Hilliard rolled them on the bed, then slipped his hand down his back and over his ass. He whimpered when Hilliard tapped his entrance, a finger teasing the skin. Brian was on fucking fire—he wished Hilliard would hurry the hell up. He didn't need slow and patient. Tonight he wanted fast and furious. Hilliard humphed, and Brian caught a glimpse of the foil pouch. He grabbed it and tore it open as he sat up and straddled Hilliard's legs.

He rolled the condom down Hilliard's long, thick cock and then got into position, slowly lowering himself halfway to heaven. Brian paused, and Hilliard tugged him down into a deep kiss that rocked Brian's world. Then, slowly, they began to move together. It was intense, with Hilliard breathing deeply in his ear and Brian holding on to Hilliard, afraid he was going to fly into a million pieces at any second.

Pulling away, Brian groaned and cried out before Hilliard tugged him back down into another kiss. He didn't know how long he was going to be able to take this. He was so full, and Hilliard seemed to touch his heart from the inside and his soul with his eyes. He had never felt so cared for and special. Brian never wanted this feeling to end, so he closed his eyes and sank into himself, letting the sensation wash over him.

For a few minutes, it was easy just to exist outside his own body, floating on waves of pleasure that Hilliard kept building until he pulled Brian right back with him, desire slamming him in the chest hard. Yet they continued rocking together, their movements never missing a beat, like Hilliard knew exactly what Brian needed. When to press and when to back off. "Hill… I need…."

"I know," he breathed. "I do too." He held Brian tighter, their movements growing more frantic. Brian held on, letting Hilliard guide the ride. Brian gasped as he slammed his eyes closed, his cock sliding between himself and Hilliard, getting just enough friction to keep him on the edge but not enough to send him over it. "But not yet." He cupped Brian's cheeks, holding him tightly, their gazes locking.

"I'm…." His head pounded, and he needed to come.

Hilliard drew his face close to him. "Then come for me. I know it's what you want, and I want to feel you." He drove upward, and Brian's spine felt like it was on fire. He shook as pressure built from deep inside. Unable to control his own body, Brian gave himself over to the sensation, spilling his release between them. Hilliard slammed up into him, holding still as he too came unglued, holding Brian tightly.

Neither of them moved as they held each other, breathing deeply, letting the warmth wash over them. Brian's brain felt fried, and the last thing he wanted was to try to think. He lay still, holding Hilliard.

Finally he said, "Do you think we can do that again?"

"Yeah… definitely, but maybe not right away," Hilliard whispered. "I'm going to need some time. Maybe give me ten minutes and we'll see if we can go for another round."

Brian snickered and then groaned as Hilliard slipped out of him. "Maybe we're going to need more time than that."

"In the morning, then." Hilliard stood up and took care of the condom before returning. They cleaned up quickly and settled in bed once more. Hilliard rolled on his side, slipping his arm around Brian and pulling him close as the sounds of the night and ocean peacefully invaded the room. Brian was happy, really happy, and he didn't want to go to sleep because this feeling didn't tend to stick around for long, and he wanted to enjoy it.

Chapter 17

HE WAS so content. The sun filled the room with light, Brian lay still in his arms where he'd been the entire night, and everything was okay. They had caught the person who had framed him and had more than enough evidence to clear Brian's name. And to top it off, Hilliard had a vision of his future, and it all revolved around this house and this man. He sighed, because six months ago, he never would have dreamed that he would feel like this—happy. Fucking *happy*.

A sharp knock downstairs pulled him out of his reverie. Brian didn't move, which was good. Carefully, Hilliard slipped out of bed. He pulled on a light pair of sweats and a T-shirt, heading down as the knock sounded again.

"What is it now?" Hilliard asked with a yawn as he opened the door to Uncle Timothy's hulking form. "I got your little fantasy missive and have already forwarded it to Aunt Grace's lawyer." He shrugged. "Too bad it has no basis. We're moving for a dismissal because the suit has no merit."

"You think so," he growled and slapped a piece of paper into Hilliard's hand. "Grace signed the house over to me before she died."

Hilliard looked at the paper before rolling his eyes. "First thing, it takes more than a scrawled handwritten piece of paper and a signature to transfer real estate. Where are the witnesses and the notary signatures? This was obviously made up two days ago after you left." He shook his head. "Aunt Grace's will was very clear. The lawyer did a title search, and there are no claims or anything like that. Real estate transactions need to be registered with the state and filed in the county. Was any of that done?" He had been studying real estate law and procedure for the past week, so all this information was fresh in his mind. "I can call the sheriff, and he can take a look at this. If it's fake, then you'll end up in jail rather than in this house." Hilliard was more than a little sick of this man and his self-entitlement. "Besides, because of her will, you will need to prove that she changed her mind, especially after what was said in the document."

Timothy yanked the page back, folded it, and jammed it into his pocket. "You little piece of shit. You came in here and turned my mother against me." He pushed forward. Hilliard was a little stunned as his uncle knocked him aside and nearly sent him to the floor. "So help me God, I will get you out of this house if I have to carry you out piece by piece."

"What the heck is going on?" Brian hurried down the stairs in a pair of boxers… and nothing else. His skin shone, and as he reached the bottom of the stairs, he turned to Timothy. "I already called the police. I heard the threats you made. That will be more than enough." He stalked toward Timothy, and Hilliard wondered if the two were going to break into a fight in his living room.

"Don't." Hilliard placed his hand on Brian's arm. "He isn't worth it. Bullies are never worth it." He stepped forward, meeting his uncle's gaze. "You come in here with some dubious paperwork that can be easily disproved and what? You think I'm just going to walk away?" He breathed deeply, anger rising. "I see why Aunt Grace left me the house. You're an ass. I bet you treated your mother like crap and then expected her to give you everything you wanted." He was so tired of people like Timothy. Alan had treated him the same way much of the time, and Hilliard had just let him. When he didn't get his way, Alan had bullied and cajoled until he got it, and Hilliard had no one to blame for that but himself.

"You pansy-assed little—" Uncle Timothy lunged forward, trying to tackle him. Hilliard jumped out of the way, tripping his uncle, who crashed to the floor just as Grant hurried inside.

"I saw him come at you through the window," Grant said, already in action, holding Timothy to the floor. "What happened?"

"He came here trying to intimidate Hilliard. What he expected to get is beyond us. Maybe the guy is just crazy," Brian added. "Oh, and he has a document he tried to use to say that the house was signed over to him. It's likely fake."

Grant got the paper and looked it over. "So we can add fraud to the assault charges." He smiled, and Timothy growled and thrashed on the floor like a large landed fish.

"I'll look into all of this," Grant said before calling for backup. He kept Timothy on the floor until another deputy arrived, and then they took him away.

"Well, that was exciting. More statements we're going to need to make."

Brian drew closer. "At least the police procedure section of the exam should be a breeze." He grinned, and Hilliard tugged Brian into a kiss before hugging him tightly.

"I'm so tired of this crap. I just want him to go away, and I want to be able to start my new life here." Nothing was ever easy. "I want us to be able to get on with things." He rested his head on Brian's shoulder. "But it will get there, I know that. It just takes time." He wondered if he was reassuring himself or Brian.

"That's what you keep telling me whenever I ask how long it will take before I'm officially cleared. Everything takes time." He held Hilliard closer, and they stood together in the quiet, which was broken by a car speeding way too fast down the road. Brian went to the window and peered out, shaking his head. "Figures...."

"Frank's kids?" Hilliard asked.

"And their friends." Brian let the curtains fall back into place. Hilliard stilled, meeting Brian's gaze. "You don't think...."

"Yeah. Why not?" Hilliard asked. "Do you know where those friends live?"

Brian went back to the window, and Hilliard followed. "See that red house between the town and the cliffs? One of them lives there. I did some work on the outside a few months ago. The siding takes a beating from the spray and salt air. It took me forever to get paid."

Hilliard nodded. "You know, since they're clients, maybe you should pay them a visit and see if they have any additional work for you. Maybe we can talk to the family. Kids talk all the time, and sometimes they have no idea what to keep to themselves. So what if Kevin or Kendall accidentally mentioned to their friends where their grandmother kept stuff? Kids brag, or they let things slip...."

"Okay. Let me get dressed, and then we can pay them a visit. Though I don't know what we can expect."

Hilliard scratched his head. "I don't know either, but we have to try to find out."

Brian shook his head. "No, we really don't. We can let the police look into this. We got what we needed."

Hilliard sat down. "You're probably right. We could just let them handle it." He glanced up at Brian, who shook his head and rolled his eyes.

"You can't just walk away, can you."

"Would you…?" Hilliard suddenly stopped. His mouth hanging open, and then he clamped it shut. "Sorry. You wouldn't want me to just quit, would you?"

Brian drew closer. "That isn't what you were going to say." His gaze bored into him. "You were about to say something very different and you stopped. What was it?"

Hilliard swallowed hard. "Just let it go. I was about to run my mouth, and that's a bad thing for someone like me. I get into trouble…."

Brian drew even nearer, his face right up next to Hilliard's. "Just tell me."

He sighed. "I was about to say would you love me if I just quit?" He looked away. "I know it was stupid. Can we just forget it?"

Brian placed a finger under his chin, bringing his face back forward. "You're probably right. I think I first fell in love with your conviction, and even when I had doubts piled halfway to the sky, you never stopped and knew we'd find something. So yeah, I love you for that… and so much more." He smiled.

Hilliard's mouth went dry. Brian loved him. Damn, just hearing the words made his heart soar. "I love you too," he half croaked. "You reduced a lawyer to near speechlessness." He held Brian to him, closing his eyes just to take in this moment so he would always remember it. What he really wanted to do was pull Brian back upstairs, strip him down, and make love until they could barely move.

Brian was much more practical. "So yeah, let's go pay a visit and see if we find something. But after this, can we let it go? The police are better able to handle this sort of thing than we are. You and I can go on with our lives and be happy."

Hilliard loved that idea. He had to admit he didn't think anything was going to come of this either, but he had to give it a try. "Okay. After this we back away and let Grant do his thing. It isn't like there's much chance of anyone finding out anything at this point. Frank has muddied the waters to the point that any trail is likely tainted by him anyway." He hated giving up, but Hilliard had to admit that he had already accomplished his real goal. "Let's stop by Beverly's and take the dogs with us. I'm sure they could use a walk, and it would seem less threatening."

Brian nodded, and they headed out. At Beverly's, the dogs were excited to go out, and Beverly seemed on cloud nine, smiling from ear to ear. "Gran…?" Brian queried.

"You hush," Beverly told him. "Take the dogs for a walk." She shooed them out, and Hilliard and Brian headed out along the flats toward the ocean.

"What do you expect to gain from this?" Brian asked.

Hilliard shrugged. "I'm hoping that if Nathan is home, we can talk to him." Hilliard smiled when he saw a bike near the house. It was the one that had passed when the kids dirtied up his car. He walked more quickly, the dogs excited to be out.

No one seemed to be around when they approached the house, but he and Brian went right up the walk and knocked firmly. He was thinking about what he was going to ask when the door opened.

"What do you want?" a kid that must have been Nathan asked. He had the California surfer look down to a T, with long bleach-blond hair, blue eyes, and a T-shirt and cutoffs.

"To talk to you," Hilliard said.

Nathan shook his head. "I ain't talking to you. I know what you did to Kevin and Kendall's dad." He stepped back to close the door.

"Hey," a woman said from behind Nathan. "This is my house, not yours." She reopened the door. "I'm sorry for his manners. I'm Christine West." She looked at Brian and Hilliard before smiling down at the dogs. "I don't know what we can talk to you about, though."

"I'm leaving," Nathan said, pushing past all of them and out to the car with the surfboard on the roof. "The waves are calling." He hurried away, and Hilliard watched him go.

"I'm sorry to bother you." He smiled. "Would it be too much to ask for a bowl of water for the dogs before we walk them home?" Gigi was panting a lot, and he didn't want her or Poppy to get stressed. This whole thing was a fool's errand. Hilliard was no detective like those people on television. Heck, they were just fictional characters, and yet somehow he thought that if he talked to enough people, the solution to this mystery would present itself. He didn't know what he expected, but he should have listened to Brian and just let Grant do his job. Hilliard felt like a fool, at least to himself. But Brian gently touched his arm and smiled at him.

"Sure, come on in. They look like sweet dogs." She stepped back, and the dogs led the way in like the princesses they were. "My deadbeat ex-husband was allergic to animals, so Nathan and I could never have pets when he was growing up. Now I suppose I could have one, but I guess I never got around to getting one." She bent over to give each of the dogs a scratch. "Let me get some bowls." She left them in the living room and went into the big kitchen just beyond. "I'm sorry about Nathan. He's really a good boy. After his father left us for some floozy in his office, it's just been the two of us." Water ran, and Hilliard looked around the room.

The furniture had seen better days. It was worn but looked comfortable, just like the house. It was clean and well cared for. Hilliard guessed that money was tight and had been for a while. He understood about just hanging on. He'd done plenty of it when he was younger.

The walls were covered in what looked like original, if maybe amateurish, paintings and pictures of Nathan as he grew up. Everywhere he looked, a smiling face shone down, a few with missing front teeth.

"What are you doing?" Brian whispered as Hilliard went to take a closer look at a picture that had been enlarged and now hung in the center of the main wall. It was one of Nathan surfing.

"That was taken when Nathan won the junior championship out in Hawaii," his mother said. Hilliard turned as she set the bowls on the mat near the door. The dogs immediately began drinking. Hilliard looked back to the picture.

"How long ago was that?"

"A little over two years. I could never have afforded to send him, let alone go along, but Nathan won a place, and the organization was so excited to have him that they paid for the whole trip." She beamed as she told the story, but Hilliard was barely paying attention. A long shelf ran under the picture. It held a couple of trophies, a small bottle of sand, a Hummel child in a swing, and two small detailed figurines that had yellowed with age. "Nathan gave those to me after we got back." She must have seen him admiring the small pieces. "To thank me, I guess." The way she beamed told Hilliard plenty about how she felt about her son.

"Thank you for getting the dogs some water. We really appreciate it," Brian said from behind him. The dogs had lain down on the floor. Nathan's mom picked up the bowls and took them to the kitchen as Hilliard headed for the door. When she returned, she once again looked toward the picture on the wall.

"That was the happiest time in Nathan's life," she told them. A kettle whistled in the kitchen, and she went to deal with it.

Hilliard pulled out his phone and took a couple of quick pictures while looking like he was checking something. The whistle stopped and she returned. She saw them to the door, and Hilliard thanked her again for being so good to the dogs before they stepped out into the morning.

"I guess that was a waste of time," Brian said softly as they walked back toward town. "I need to get to work or I'll never get what I need to done." He strode toward Beverly's at a fast pace, with Hilliard struggling to keep up. Brian stopped outside the gate at the front walk, breathing heavily, glaring at Hilliard. "What is so interesting on your phone?" His gaze narrowed.

"Let's go inside," Hilliard said, leading Brian up the walk.

"Mrs. Weller called and was asking when you'd be by. I told her about eleven," Gran told Brian, who relaxed a little. "I knew you two were up to something."

"Not much. Just a trip down Nathan memory lane for Mrs. West. She was nice enough to give the dogs water."

"She did more than that," Hilliard said.

"Excuse me?" Brian sat on the sofa, and Hilliard sat next to him, the dogs each taking a lap.

Hilliard pulled out his phone and enlarged one of the pictures. "These two small figurines are netsukes. They're Japanese, and I'm willing to bet they were stolen from Violet. A little over two years ago, give or take, Nathan was in a junior surfing championship in Hawaii, a trip that was supposedly paid for." He held Brian's gaze as the pieces filled in.

"You mean…?"

Hilliard nodded. "Let's say that one of his friends, Kendall or Kevin, was telling surfer-boy Nathan a story about where their gran kept some of her valuables. You can even hear a joke about granny panties and stuff. Nathan goes in when Violet is at church and robs the place, knowing where some things are. He also grabs anything else that's small and looks valuable. Then he gets out of the house and goes home. Maybe he goes to San Francisco and sells the goods a few days later. Then he uses the money to take himself and his mom to Hawaii, using some grand story about the organization paying, and there you have it. The goods are gone, and he doesn't think anything of the figurines—they aren't silver or anything—so he gives the ivory pieces to his mom, saying he got them for her in Hawaii, and she puts them on the shelf in plain sight all this time."

"Jesus," Brian breathed. "Is that it?"

"Yeah. And if Frank had left well enough alone and not been so afraid that his boys had been the thieves, Nathan would have been caught some time ago. He was a suspect—"

"Until another one landed in their lap," Beverly interjected, shaking her head. "I'll call Grant, and he can check with Violet that those are her pieces. Then he can wrap this up and bring it to an end." She put her head back in her chair, looking tired. "I've dreamed of this. I knew it wasn't my Brian." She leaned forward, her eyes suddenly filled with fire. "But I swear if I get my hands on Nathan West, I'll give him the spanking he's long deserved." She got out of her chair and stalked to the kitchen. Hilliard hoped he never pissed her off, that was for sure.

Hilliard smiled and Brian sighed, leaning against him. "Thank you."

"For what?" Hilliard asked.

"Everything," he whispered. "For believing in me, for finding out about Frank, about Nathan, for standing by me...." His voice broke. "For loving me when most people thought I was a thief."

Hilliard kissed him gently. "There's no need to thank me, sweetheart. Somehow I think I got the better end of the deal." He nuzzled the spot behind Brian's ear. "I found a hot guy who is gentle, kind, and handy around the house. And he loves me." What more could he want?

Epilogue

HILLIARD GOT out of bed, careful not to wake Brian, who was stretched out next to him. With the covers kicked to the foot of the bed, his perfect bare butt was on display. He stepped to the window as winter rain fell outside, the clouds so close to the ground that everything seemed to disappear into them.

"What time is it?" Brian groaned.

"Close enough," Hilliard said softly, sitting on the edge of the bed.

Brian rolled over and then sat up. "I just got to sleep." He rubbed his eyes, and Hilliard couldn't take his gaze off him. He'd been sleeping in Hilliard's bed every night for the past three months, and Hilliard doubted he would ever get tired of that sight.

"I know, but the hearing is in two hours, so shower and get ready. I'll have your suit out for you." He pulled on sweatpants and shooed Brian to the bathroom, mostly to get his sexiness behind a closed door, otherwise they were never going to make it in time. Once the door closed, he went downstairs and made a light breakfast.

Brian joined him in sweats and a T-shirt that clung in all the right places. The man was temptation itself. But Hilliard kept his mind on the prize, and once they'd eaten, he took care of the dishes and they both got dressed in their court clothes.

Hilliard made sure the house was locked, got their umbrellas, and drove Brian to Beverly's. She was ready and waiting. Brian helped her into the car, and Hilliard dove them all to the county courthouse in Fort Bragg.

"I'm nervous," Brian said as they sat, waiting for their case to be called.

"It's okay," Hilliard said gently, squeezing Brian's hand and then letting it go as Brian's name was called. Brian kissed Beverly on the cheek, and then the two of them approached the front of the room, where the judge sat at his bench. "Hilliard Bauman, counsel for Brian Mayer, Your Honor." He couldn't help smiling. His official license to practice law in California had arrived two weeks ago, and representing Brian was his first court appearance.

"You're here to have Mr. Mayer's conviction for burglary vacated," the judge said.

"Yes, Your Honor." He waited to let the judge speak. "All of the facts regarding his wrongful conviction, as well as the arrest and apprehension of the true thief, are documented in the writ."

The judge, who had a reputation as a no-nonsense, stoic man, actually smiled. "I see that. A very thorough case. It seems you have statements from everyone, from the victim to the police." He set down the pages. "Mr. Mayer." He held Brian in his steely gaze. "I sit up here most days listening to some of the worst things that people do to one another. People in my courtroom are found either guilty or not guilty. But today I get to do something pretty rare." He smiled. "I get to declare someone innocent." He shuffled through the pages, picked up a pen, and began to write. Then he handed the papers to the clerk, who stamped them. "Mr. Mayer, you are hereby exonerated of the crime for which you were wrongly convicted." He banged his gavel with a grin. "The papers will be filed with the clerk, and she will make a copy for you to take with you today." He banged the gavel once more.

"Thank you," Brian said softly.

"Yes, thank you," Hilliard added. Then they turned, helped Beverly to her feet, and all three of them left the courtroom, the heavy doors closing behind them.

"Is that it?" Brian asked.

"Yes. All it needed was the judge's signature and that's the end of it." He smiled. "Come on. Let me get a copy of the order and we'll go. We have people who will be waiting for us back at the pub." Hilliard hugged Brian tightly. "Your grandmother put this together with everyone she knows. I think she fully intends to make sure there isn't a person in town who doesn't know that you have been officially declared innocent." He squeezed Brian to him. "We can have a little lunch and then slip away to have a celebration of our own."

Brian shivered in his arms, and then they released each other. Hilliard got a copy of the signed order before they left and drove right back into town. The pub's outdoor section had been closed off, and they were all led right out there. The space was full of people, including Ruth, Grant, and even Violet, as well as a number of people Hilliard didn't know. But everyone knew Brian, the men patting him on the back and the ladies getting a hug or a kiss on the cheek, some both.

"Are you okay?" Hilliard asked. "I know this is a mixed bag for you."

Violet patted his hand, her back as straight as steel. "Frank made his own bed, and there's little I can do for him. Kevin and Kendall are staying with me for the time being until they can find places of their own." She sighed softly.

"I'm sorry," Brian said as he slipped an arm around Hilliard's waist.

"Don't be. I should be apologizing to you." She wiped the corner of her eye.

"How about we call all of it water under the bridge and stop apologizing for things we aren't responsible for?" A server came over, and Brian got a beer for each of them. "What I want more than anything is to build a future of my own." They shared a moment.

"Hear! Hear!" Violet said, moving away when Ruth brought her over to where she was sitting.

"It's all working out in the end," Brian said to Hilliard. "And that's because of you."

A server came out from inside, pointing to Hilliard as a gray-haired man stepped out and then down the stairs. He pulled off his hat and came over. "I'm sorry to interrupt, but I heard you were here. Word around town is that you help people."

"Oh, I see. Yes. I have a legal practice here in town." He pulled out his wallet and handed the man a card. "What sort of problem is it?"

"Oh." He held the card and stared at it for a minute. "This isn't a legal matter, not strictly speaking anyway. See, I don't need a lawyer as much as someone who can solve a mystery. My house is haunted, and the ghosts are stealing from me, but nobody believes me." Hilliard thought the man might be a little off his rocker, but the fear in his eyes was real. "Do you think you can help me?"

This could be a fool's errand, but Hilliard nodded anyway. "Come by the office tomorrow. You can tell me what's happening, and I'll see what I can do to help."

The man grinned and sighed. "Thank you. I'll be there first thing." He hurried off, and Hilliard watched him go.

"You just can't help yourself, can you?" Brian said with a smirk, tugging Hillard to him.

"I became a lawyer to help people."

Brian nodded. "Heck, you proved I wasn't a thief. I suppose you can do anything."

Hilliard drew Brian right to him, their lips inches apart. "Who says you aren't a thief? After all, you stole my heart."

Keep reading for an excerpt from
New Leaf
by Andrew Grey

AFTER HOURS of talking and listening, Dex was worn out, and the time change was getting to him. Fortunately, he found Jane.

"Go for a walk. This will go on until the funeral. Your mother was loved, but it's going to be overwhelming if you don't take a break." She smiled. "Take the keys to the store if you want."

Dex gratefully went out the back door and through the yard, weaving along the back alley to the store. Then, after unlocking the rear door, he let himself inside.

The familiar scent of dust, books, and his mother nearly sent him reeling. This he remembered. Dex closed the door and turned on the lights as he wandered through the small back room with its boxes and shelves. His mother didn't keep much back here. She never had. She'd always said that she couldn't sell what was back here, so she kept as much of her stock out front as possible. Dex perused the area, remembering the corner where she'd set up a table and chairs. He had sat there for hours doing his homework, coloring, crafts—all of it in his own corner of the store. Oh, the hours he'd spent in this space with his mom. She always came back to check on him, and if there was no one in the store, she'd read to him or they'd color together until the bell on the front door jangled. It got to the point that he hated that bell because it meant she'd have to go back to work.

He peeked into some of the boxes before stepping through the curtain and out behind the register. The lights were off, but the sun shone in through the front windows. Everything looked as though his mother would return at any moment to open up. The shelves were all in order, and even the notebook she kept on the counter behind the register sat in its usual spot, surrounded by the trinkets and bookmark display. Dex lifted the counter and lowered it again once he'd stepped out from behind it, then wandered the aisles, looking over the rack of children's books. His mother had read most of them to him at one point. Of course, there were newer ones as well, but he continued on, checking over the shelves.

More books were turned cover forward to fill the shelves than he remembered. When he was a kid, the store had always been packed. But now it seemed staged—behind the single titles, there was nothing. The inventory he remembered his mother carrying wasn't in the store. Maybe it was just the children's section?

He continued to the adult areas of the store. There he found only a few hardcover books, and of the titles she had, his mother only had two or three copies. Dex knew independent bookstores had been having a difficult time in the past years because of Amazon, but every time he had asked his mother how the store was, she had told him it was fine. Maybe things hadn't been as rosy as his mother projected.

A knock on the front door startled him. He went up front, turned the lock, and opened the door. "Can I help you? We're closed for the next few days."

"I'm sorry. I was just passing, and I always stop by when I'm downtown." The man lifted his gaze, and Dex was struck by the most intensely blue eyes he had ever seen.

"My mother passed away and…." Damn, it was hard just to say the words. "The store will be closed until after the funeral." He put his hand over his mouth, willing himself not to fall apart. He had been okay a few minutes ago, but the grief was suddenly too much to bear.

"I'm so sorry. She was a nice lady." He paused, lowering his gaze slightly, looking like he might leave. "You're Sarah's son? She talked a lot about you. She said you were going to be in the movies." He smiled.

Dex swallowed hard. His mind skipped to how hunkalicious this guy was, with his hair all askew and his wrinkled shirt open just enough to allow Dex to catch a glimpse of a smattering of brown chest hair.

"Yes. I'm Dex." It was nice that his mom had talked about him. Even if he hadn't had any real success in Hollywood, his mother had always been proud of him anyway, he thought, his heart hitching.

"I was a regular customer of your mom's. I try to support local businesses, and she'd order in the books I wanted. That way she got the business instead of the big online places." He smiled, and Dex nodded.

"Did she have an order for you?" He wondered where his mother might have put it if she had.

"No. There were a few books I wanted, though. Still, I can come back once you're open again…." He leaned closer. "You are opening again, aren't you?" The blue in his eyes grew darker. "This is the only place in town that would order books for me. At least, the ones I wanted." He looked up and down the street. "I've got a weakness for romance— the masculine kind."

"I see…."

He put his hand over his mouth. "Of course. Sarah told me she had a gay son." He cleared his throat. "I'm sorry. I'm Les. Les Gable." He shook his hand. "I'm sorry to keep you. I'll come back later." He paused. "I just want to tell you that your mom was the greatest. She cared so much about everyone. I'm going to miss her." Then he turned and, with a wave, hurried down the sidewalk.

Dex closed the door and locked it again. It seemed his mother had had an impact on a lot of people in town. She had always loved books and got a great deal of joy from reading, something she had passed on to Dex.

He walked through the store before returning to the back room. He found the safe where his mother always kept it, and searched his memory for the combination. She had told him what it was years ago, and luckily the numbers returned to him. He opened it and peered inside, where he found less than a hundred dollars, her starting bank for the day. He also pulled out the store accounts book. Then he closed the safe door and locked it again.

He wasn't sure what else he wanted to do, but he didn't want to go back to the house. The grief gathering was probably still going on, and he'd had enough. His mother was gone, and Dex needed to try to process the loss alone. He didn't need dozens of people talking about his mother for him to know her. His mom was here in this building—in each book, as well as in the way she'd painted each wall a different color because she thought it would be cheerful. The only problem was that she'd picked the brightest colors possible. Dex was afraid his eyes would start bleeding if he didn't do something about it soon. Especially that grass-green carpeting. "Mom, I love you, but your decorating was a nightmare," he said out loud, smiling. That was his mother. She loved what she loved, and to hell with what everyone else thought.

Dex set down the books and headed for the bathroom, gasping when he opened the door. Apparently where the bathroom in the house was Whoville, the one in the store was all Alice in Wonderland, and it had gotten the same treatment, including a Mad Hatter toilet-paper holder and a Queen of Hearts toilet cozy. The White Rabbit bounded over one of the walls, but it was Alice being sucked down the rabbit hole that made him laugh. It came with a reminder to flush. This was his mother in a nutshell. She could be out there, and yet she could also be so clever.

He shut the door, unable to use the bathroom, and retrieved the record book. It was time to go back to the house. At least now he could review his mom's records and figure out if it was viable to keep the store going.

He had a task to accomplish, something that would fill some hours and keep him from moping around. If the store was his mother's legacy, Dex needed to see if there was a way to move forward. He pulled open the rear door and locked it behind him, then headed back toward the house.

He decided to take a roundabout route, walking down to the square as the clock in the old courthouse chimed the hour. He paused and smiled. He remembered being in the store, listening for that bell, because most days, when it chimed six times, his mom would close up and they would go home. He shook his head as if to clear the memories. Something around every corner seemed to remind him of her. The trees had all leafed out, shading the streets. Dex wiped his eyes. In his mind's eye, he could see his mom and dad in their backyard, music drifting out from the house as they danced to a cascade of flower petals.

At the time, he'd considered it horribly embarrassing, especially when his mother had backed away from his dad insisting that she teach Dex to dance. Dex had fought it with everything he had. He hadn't wanted to learn to dance. But she'd made him. Damn, what he wouldn't give to dance with her with one last time.

"Dex?"

He turned and once again met Les's blue eyes. His heart beat a little faster and his throat dried in an instant, especially seeing the heat and interest in those eyes. Dex was used to people looking at him with hunger, but this was something more. "I just left the library and was on my way back to my apartment. What are you up to?"

"I finished up in the store and figured it was time to go home." He nodded in the direction he was going, and Les fell into step along with him, walking slowly. Dex realized that his one leg seemed stiff. He shortened his usual stride so Les wouldn't have to strain to keep up.

Les smiled at him. "Sarah always told me stories about you when I was in the store. She said that you're an actor working in LA."

"I haven't been working all that much lately, unfortunately. Unless you count porn," Dex said, his voice deadpan.

Les stopped midstride. "You did porn?"

Dex shook his head, grinning. "Oh God, no. My last audition was supposed to be a serious role, but well, it didn't turn out that way. My mother was always supportive, but I can't help but think her support would not stretch to cover that." He chuckled. "Though maybe Mom would have just told me to do my best, then rented a copy later so she could tell me what I'd done wrong." He chuckled. "I would have to say that the most embarrassing thing I can think of is my mother going out to get a copy of Shaving Ryan's Privates or something, so she could rate my performance."

Les chuckled. "It must have been nice to have that kind of support in your life. I never did. My family wasn't anywhere near as open-minded as your mom, that's for sure. My folks were very predictable. 'You will go to college, you will go to church, you will not be gay or have gay thoughts.'" The humor left his voice and his posture became more rigid when he spoke of his parents.

Dex had always known he'd been lucky, especially when it came to his mom, but he sometimes forgot how fortunate. "I never knew how Mom was going to take anything. You remember what it was like to be a teenager and all you wanted to do was shock your parents? I'd do that, and Mom would look at me and say, 'It's okay, I support you and will always love you.' Then the next day she'd decide that the upstairs bathroom needed painting and I'd walk in and get a surprise of my own when the walls were jet black… or neon yellow. The hall bathroom upstairs has been both at one time. I think it was her way of shocking me right back. And her offbeat decorating skills usually did the trick."

Les laughed out loud, his stance loosening. "She would do the funniest things. One time when I came into the store, she had the shelves pulled back from one of the walls and was painting it Barbie pink, just so she could see how it would look."

"That's my mom," Dex agreed.

"At least she liked color. My mother painted the entire house this off-white color. She called it Palest Peony or something, and every wall in every room was the same color, all through the house. I had to beg her to let me do my room in blue. She eventually let me, but only if I promised that if it didn't work out, I'd paint it back. The furniture was every shade of brown, and the carpet beige. It was like living in a forest in permanent winter. Mom's idea of adding color was bringing in black accents… because they went with everything." Les began to laugh. "My dad hated it. So for Christmas, he used to get her really bright knickknacks. They would be on display for a while and then suddenly they'd disappear." He smiled.

"You're kidding, right?" Dex asked. When Les shook his head, Dex added, "You should see the guest bedroom upstairs. It has this psychedelic wallpaper, as if the person who created it had done acid back in the sixties. I have no idea where Mom found it, but I'm surprised anyone who's stayed over hasn't suffered from seizures." He paused. "You know, that could be why Mom didn't get many guests. They'd stay one night and detour to the hospital on their way out of town."

Les shrugged, smiling. "You know what they say—after three days, both fish and guests begin to stink. Maybe it was her way of controlling the odor." He tilted his head adorably to the side, and Dex took a second to enjoy the view. Les had a strong jaw and an expressive face that pulled Dex in. His high cheekbones gave him an almost regal look, and yet his eyes danced with mischief. And he had a sense of humor, which was necessary… if just to get through the trials and tribulations of life. Dex had definitely needed one with his mother. She had sometimes been a handful.

"My mom's guest room…."

"Let me guess, slightly pinky off-white," Dex teased.

"Yup. I remember having a friend for a sleepover. I showed him into the room—he set down his bag and fell onto the bed, asleep instantly." He grinned and Dex rolled his eyes before chuckling lightly.

"So your mom was color-challenged. And mine was a color ninja, never afraid of anything." They approached the house, and Dex groaned as a couple went inside carrying a casserole dish. "I swear to God, the house is going to explode with all the grief food people are bringing." He patted his stomach, which did a little roll at the thought. "Want to hazard a guess as to the number of pounds of macaroni and cans of soup that have given their lives already?"

Les shook his head vehemently. "Not on your life." He patted Dex's shoulder, and heat spread through him from the touch. "I need to get home too. But I'll see you later at the store?" His gaze met Dex's, and Dex nodded but made no effort to move away. There was something incredibly attractive about being lost in those eyes, and he was in no hurry to return to reality. Les licked his lips, and just like that, Dex wondered how he tasted. Les was a feast for the eyes, and his musky scent wafted on the breeze. Dex swallowed hard, wishing for more, but there were limits to what he'd do with a guy he'd just met.

It was bad enough that Dex had done things he could never tell his mother in order to try to secure a role. He suppressed a shiver thinking about it. This wasn't Hollywood. Les was just a handsome guy. "I should go inside and make sure Jane isn't overwhelmed."

Les nodded, and Dex shook his hand, then forced himself to turn away from him and walk inside the house.

Scan the QR code below to order

ANDREW GREY is the author of more than two hundred works of Contemporary Gay Romantic fiction, including an Amazon Editors Best Romance of 2023. After twenty-seven years in corporate America, he has now settled down in Central Pennsylvania with his husband of more than twenty-five years, Dominic, and his laptop. An interesting ménage. Andrew grew up in western Michigan with a father who loved to tell stories and a mother who loved to read them. Since then he has lived throughout the country and traveled throughout the world. He is a recipient of the RWA Centennial Award, has a master's degree from the University of Wisconsin–Milwaukee, and now writes full-time. Andrew's hobbies include collecting antiques, gardening, and leaving his dirty dishes anywhere but in the sink (particularly when writing). He considers himself blessed with an accepting family, fantastic friends, and the world's most supportive and loving partner. Andrew currently lives in beautiful, historic Carlisle, Pennsylvania.

Email: andrewgrey@comcast.net
Website: www.andrewgreybooks.com

ANDREW GREY
Love
AT FIRST SWIPE

Darby Wright has fought for his independence ever since he lost his sight as a child. But even now that he has his own home and a good job, his overprotective mother doesn't believe he can handle himself. Darby's determined to prove her wrong, but there are some things—like finding his guide dog's potty accident—where an extra set of eyes would come in handy.

Enter See For Me, an app that connects blind clients with sighted volunteers. See For Me is designed for just this sort of emergency, and it's through this app that Darby meets Reynaldo. Lust at first voice turns to more when Darby and Reynaldo run into each other at a local sandwich shop, where Renaldo seems as nice in person as he was in app.

With Reynaldo, Darby can feel his world expanding. Reynaldo doesn't just support him but understands him and sees Darby as more than his disability. But will being with Reynaldo mean giving up Darby's hard-fought independence, or will it mean gaining something more than he ever dreamed?

Scan the QR code below to order

How can they be together when
they live in different worlds?

The Duke's Cowboy

COWBOY NOBILITY ♥ BOOK ONE

ANDREW GREY

Cowboy Nobility: Book One

George Lester, the Duke of Northumberland, flees familial expectations in Britain for the promise of freedom of San Francisco, looking for the chance to be himself. But before he even gets close, a blizzard forces him off the road, and he finds himself freezing half to death in a small town with no motel… with a litter of puppies to look after.

Luckily for George, he also finds Alan.

As the heir to his family's ranch, Alan Justice knows the burden of being the oldest son. He doesn't have time to show George, the stranger his brother dragged home, what it takes to be a cowboy. But that very night, George surprises him by helping a mare in distress through a difficult birth. Maybe the duke is made of sterner stuff than Alan thought.

George and Alan keep surprising each other, and every day they grow a little closer. But when George's responsibilities call him home, Alan finds he's the one who has something to prove—that he can handle what it means to be the duke's cowboy.

Scan the QR code below to order

DEDICATED
TO YOU
ANDREW GREY

Dillon Fitzgerald is a famous singer. He's also exhausted. Too many shows in a too busy schedule have left too little time for him to write or relax. He feels like the music is being strangled out of him. Some time is just what the doctor ordered, so when his friend offers him a week on a cruise, Dillon gets right on board. All he has to do is grow a little beard and hope no one recognizes him.

Financial advisor Tio Smythe-Barrett has been friends with Dillon forever. When the latest in a long string of girlfriends turns out to be a cheater, Tio offers her spot on what would have been a romantic vacation to Dillon instead. After all, why wouldn't he want to spend a week with his best friend?

As Tio and Dillon share close quarters, the boundaries in their friendship shift like the ocean currents. Spending time with Tio has Dil-lon's creative muse singing, and he can no longer deny that his feelings for Tio go beyond friendship. His heart soars when Tio responds to his flirting—but is he willing to risk what they have for the chance at true love?

Scan the QR code below to order

FOR **MORE**

OF THE

BEST

GAY

ROMANCE